Star Freezer

Star Freezer

GREGORY GARCIA

LitPrime Solutions
21250 Hawthorne Blvd
Suite 500, Torrance, CA 90503
www.litprime.com
Phone: 1-800-981-9893

Published by LitPrime Solutions   11/08/2021

ISBN: 978-1-955944-37-3(sc)
ISBN: 978-1-955944-38-0(e)

Library of Congress Control Number: 2021923100

Contents

David

He was sure he was alone there except for the uncanny, recently springing up, north polar wildlife lurking around, which he wanted to take photographs of and identify, but at a safe distance for him. He was well prepared to traipse the beach area on that freezing evening. He was there documenting any new changes in the natural environment. He took photos of the beach, water and soil samples, and temperature readings. He wished he had a Geiger counter to use, maybe the radiation measurements would paint him a better picture of the eerie changes there. He would do his sample collecting whenever he felt safe to do so.

Very little remained of this village David grew up in. The villagers all left fed up of the unnatural, chilly weather that occurred over the last two years. Their village always had a hot tropical climate, and the cold that crept up on them, felt like an insidious curse. The cold snaps would promptly sap vitality and change even the lightest heart to a glum mood. The residents would cringe at the heavy, unbreakable jinx they felt there.

David witnessed five hundred souls leave their home in Matelot, over a year period, but was still struck by the empty expanse he peered into. The village no longer had bustling groups gossiping, parents carrying food home to cook for their children, or even unpleasant old men cussing each other outside the bar. He beheld only empty houses which were quickly rotting and being pushed over by strange dark tree trunks - with mangling, vicious, leafless, iron branches. The people that made up the numbers in the village now were the few hardy drug dealers and the forty or so brainwashed members of a cult, that settled in the church in Matelot many years ago.

David's village of Matelot is a small fishing settlement to the north-east of Trinidad. In Matelot the furthest road ends lonely, unmarked, rutted and narrow on a cliff facing the Caribbean Sea. The needs of the people which left there in droves were simple; thirty kilometers of good road, strong retaining walls, some buses to take them to Toco at least, and warm natural sunlight. Food in the form of fish and provisions were once easy to get there, before the water became too cold, loathsome, and mind altering.

Part of David was happy when he had seen his next-door neighbors leave two weeks ago. Their house was so close David could smell the reek of their dog's urine, hear the hound's ear bleeding and chest splitting barking, and hear his neighbors bray their children's name; who would only answer after the eleventh time. In Matelot everybody knew all the minutiae about each other; which tanty was a closet alcoholic, which husband had erectile dysfunction, which children were 'duncy heads', and which neighbor worked black magic on who.

David first learned to surf there in Matelot some years ago, as a teenager, when the water was still safe and warm. He still had his seven feet funboard. He feared going into the water there now; as it would cause blanks in his memory, copious dark hallucinations, with a sprinkling of harrowing dreams. He got his first surfboard at thirteen, from an American man, who was visiting with his family in Matelot. David caught crabs and fresh fish for them which the American family greatly appreciated. He showed them the ideal places to swim and rented his uncle's pirogue to them; which they toured some of the coast with. He made them feel safe and welcome in the village. The American and his two sons taught him how to surf and left a surfboard for him, in gratitude for the superb time they enjoyed. They especially adored his sometimes-wacky Trinidadian accent. Sometimes they had to pretend that they grasp what he said. That August he learned how different his environment was to a major city in North America. The thirteen-year-old David had warm water, blue skies all year round, and fresh coconuts; whereas the cities, the American spoke about had snowplows, subway systems and apple pies. The Americans said they all had guns back home. They said it was their right to own arms. The young David had only seen guns in the movies or holstered on policemen in Matelot. David learned self sufficiency at a tender age growing up in a fishing village. His teenage years were filled with exploits of hunting, hiking and fishing. Even back then, at thirteen, he was tall with an athletic body. David was a good-looking Afro-Trinidadian with dark skin with a bald fade haircut. He was thirty-two years old now. He thought *too unyielding to leave Matelot, but too young to get my marble kaks by this brutal force coming.*

David was not immune to the dark and cold, and because of that, he had lost his enthusiasm for a lot of things he once enjoyed there. The poison there was creeping on; some malignant shadow loomed over the place. Yet bravely, or unwisely he was hoping to save the village, in which he was born. He knew he was still in Matelot, Trinidad, but everything was mutated and almost sinister now. The mango trees were gone, most bushes were alien, the birds he knew were silent and even the many mangy stray dogs; that scratched and drooled at every corner were missing. There was not even the pygmy owl's nocturnal 'hoo hoo hoo!' which made the elderly people tremble in their beds; because they were convinced that the bird was calling death for them.

David had to change the alternator belt in his van, so he had no choice but to plod to Ma Ethelrida's house today, wary of all the dangers. He brought his old silver vintage torchlight, but he forgot to change the low battery. He admonished himself for the slip up because not even the moonlight beamed there to make his steps safe and sure. If the flashlight had cut off, he resolved to just shake it violently until it would shine again. To save his ankle from twisting on the pothole-filled road, he wore his good hiking boots. He had his bush machete in a sturdy leather sack slung over his shoulder if he had to defend himself from the new animals prowling Matelot. The machete could shave his coconuts, cut low branches in his way, or cut the head of an attacking beast clean off. He panned his half-dead, pathetic, yellow light around, but he could perceive little, since a heavy veil of darkness reigned supreme there. The evening was inky with the few streetlights on the roads; which were broken or flickering dimly - like David's dream of surviving his village. It was December there, but still the little feeble day light varnished too fast, from about four in the afternoon. He felt fortunate that he knew the short road he was on like he knew his van; which was parked by Ma Ethelrida's house. When he got there he would have better lighting and repair his old van.

Trinidad never had any snow or winter season. It was supposed to have two main conditions; a wet period and a dry period. Trinidad is a naturally baking hot island, only 700 miles from the Earth's equator. But David's village was different; it would be in the thirties Celsius during the day for the rest of the island, but incrementally colder for the Matelot area. Something abhorrent was chilling the air in his village. Recently he found that near the beach the temperature would plunge unnaturally to ten degrees celsius; which is not cold for northern peoples but freezing for most Caribbean people. David had never left Trinidad so all he knew was the heat of this island. The hot sun once burned his face and arms, but the heat forgot to warm his village anymore; it was an aloof memory now.

David worked as a taxi driver in Matelot. His first car, a Datson 120Y, was repossessed by the bank, since he could not make the payments. He bought his current van from a damaged car lot. The car salesman told him "yuh like headache, tha van is rel chubble to bring back boss man!" The previous owner had drunk too much rum and flipped the van. David skillfully, like a surgeon, replaced the hood of the van and the driver side fender; and made it road worthy again. He was proud of the work he did on the van. His route was now from Shark River, where the Bailey bridge fell, to Matelot River. It is ironic that in these last days his trade was finally in a boon time. Everyone who was leaving Matelot wanted his van to transport their possessions out; antique murky varnish tri-fold vanities, hernia inducing stoves with sticky, finger sinking, unsavory layers of loathsome baked on grease, or the odd case or two of empty beer bottles. But his lavish earnings were nothing to gloat about when the whole village would be emptied out.

He wanted to believe that there are lots of Trinidadians who if given a forewarning of the approaching doomsday, would sacrifice their life; like he was willing to do for the survival of his planet. It was a suicide mission to stay there to fight the approaching calamity. He trained and prepared to face the imminent danger. He didn't want to be a hero, he thought of Jesus in the bible saying *Father, if you are willing, take this cup from me.*

From the books he and Ma Ethelrida discussed he knew first world nations had invincible armies which invaded vulnerable countries; to steal resources, kill millions and leave deadly radiation all over the planet. He learned to value his morality over material gains. He read about the past history of different political systems; communism, fascism, socialism, democracy and republic. He found that he could see eye to eye with the republic form of government.

To protect what little he had he made a bow gun; using the flat steel strip of a carpenter's square and strung with an old printer's cable. It shot welding rods, but not very far. He had to use it on a burglar once, but he thought he missed his mark. He thought about getting some real guns, but it would have no stopping power against the entity he had to fight. He grew up Catholic like most people in the village, but then became an atheist. Because he had prayed for his parents to survive an accident, and they never survived; so, he left the church on his own and he stopped believing in god. When he went to church functions, he heard the cry 'amen' after the prayer; the name of an Egyptian god whom he did not want to worship. Then the song that might be sung, in the church, would be about 'bringing the sheep'. He was not comfortable with man having the characteristics of a sheep. He was certain it would lead to a grotesque master-slave relationship. However, he did not stay an atheist. After a few years as an atheist Ma Ethelrida had balanced his mind. She told him science did not have all the answers, "it was surely limited in what it can tell you" she said. She asked him "if the universe was seventy one percent dark energy, plus twenty four percent dark matter, what we really know using science boi, eh?" He formed his own mature view of God now. His conclusion on the divine nature of the universe was that *God is within me, and very personal; and everyone around me is also part of the ocean of consciousness; fulfilling God's plan.* He didn't agree that mankind was a cosmic accident, because then that accident could be destroyed without any loss of morality by the destroyer. And from now on he would always believe that he was born with natural rights from his God.

He sensed with all his awareness evil taking over his home. He believed the brumal future predicted for his forgotten village. A great calamity was imminent, on the scale of the biblical flood. For over a year he had been living a disciplined life based on a disquieting prophecy given to him. He was encouraged not to fear the adversity and suffering as it would cleanse his soul.

David froze in fear when he spotted one of the drug dealers – narcos, called Brent pointing an Uzi at him. David's stomach knotted with fear. He knew it was too late to run even in the dim light he could not escape the rapid Uzi fire. From behind another gruff narco called Danny handled David's bush machete and slid it menacingly out of its sack. Now David was very much at their mercy. Danny slapped David hard on his back with the broad side of the machete. David shreiked in pain. He began to shake hysterically.

"You and Tants always macoing we! Yuh feel we don't know? Yuh wha we to planass yuh awah?" Brent shouted roughly, with bug eyes.

"I had to walk here, no other choice, oh God man! Hoss my van not working!" David fumbled out.

"We tell alyuh already to leave here. De boss, Djerling, will kill alyuh; you and tants. This is de last warning eh!" Brent warned. Danny pulled the camera off David.

"wha de boss go geh we for this Brent?"

"Ah doh business! Djerling go pay we in US money fuh it!" Brent replied.

Danny pulled David's insulated pouch from his shoulder.

"Yuh better have something to eat in this." Danny ramsacked the the contents of the pouche.

"Oh geed wha de ass you pee in them little bottles?" Brent spat and flung the pouche with its little bottles over his shoulders. Danny kicked the back of David's leg and David fell on his back hard. He passed out while Brent and Danny each kicked his head. David began to wake up after they left. He sat up and caressed his aching head with his hand. He knew he had to move but didn't feel his legs would carry him two steps.

He sat remembering when he was back in primary school. *One day after school David was stealing mangoes with his classmates and he did not see Ma Ethelrida coming to bolt away from her. She grabbed his hand roughly, which was holding a big rosy mango, and made David tiptoe. "Ask! Don't take! She spat infuriated by the little villain. David was so scared he could not look her in the eyes; he could only gawk at her glasses hanging on a chain down her chest. His classmates were shouting "Run! Run Bounty! But he did not hear his nickname being screamed by hysterical peers, because the shock of being caught dulled his senses. He dropped the big mango on her toes by accident. Ma Ethelrida yelped in pain and finally, after an eternity, David wrenched his had free and ran screaming along with his classmates. He never provoked Ma Ethelrida after that or stole her fruits again.*

He eventually stood up with the kind assistance of a rusty leaning fence post. He started looking for his bush machete but couldn't find it. He knew his camera was stolen for sure. He dragged his hurting body to Ma Ethelrida's house; who the drug dealers called Tants.

Ma Ethelrida

The people leaving Matelot had put the blame on Ma Ethelrida for all their woes. They complained that she was blighting their fishing nets, killing their crops, eating their pets and chilling their bones. They regularly used Ma Ethelrida as a scapegoat. If they found a strange bruise or if their limbs swelled they would say Ma Ethelrida came to their house at night, took off her skin and sucked their blood. They would sprinkle salt around their beds to try to catch her; as she would have to count all the salt grains and morning would catch her there, outside of her skin. In David's taxi they always prattled about Ma Ethelrida. Some delusional passengers rumored that she had grown so pervasive and ominous that her evil was ruining their fortunes. She was first called a witch forty years ago, soon after her husband died. Her husband had drowned at sea and his body could not be found. The people who remembered that time said Ma Ethelrida did a dark spell to find her husbands body. People saw her bare her right breast to the sea, in a ritual, and her husband's body floated up soon after. For weeks after that day the fishermen found it impossible to catch fish.

Ma Ethelrida ran the gauntlet of years of ridicule, lies and claustrophobia of the village. Anyone else would have done suicide but she persevered. Ma Ethelrida's enlightenment process was difficult but each time she would recover quickly from delirium, for the stakes were high. She saw harrowing visions of people freezing in their cars, winter wolves cornering a boy to eat him, and her charred house debris flying in frigid howling winds. Ma Ethelrida's clairvoyance increased gradually since her daughter in-law Sherlyn had disappeared, twenty years ago. To the villagers it did not feel like an important event when Sherlyn and her maniac husband had varnished. People there thought Sherlyn had only drowned in the ocean and that her husband went into hiding from the police. After their disappearance Ma Ethelrida did the hard work of discerning the evil force damning the village. She was rewarded with wisdom, while the rest of the natives continued to live with all their ignorant perceptions. When she saw the colossal decimation coming, she knew she had to forgive her tormentors or abandon her home village to its macabre fate. Despite the derision she received she boldly proclaimed the truth, without duplicity, about the coming apocalypse, to everyone around.

Two years ago, she began to share the dire warning. To talk she had to close up her little stall; where she sold healing products, she manufactured herself. After lunch she would close the two windows of her stall and cross over to the Catholic Church yard, to begin to speak. At the first attempt she shouted until her throat was sore, but no one would strain their ears to listen to her silly ranting. People easily ignored her and went about there business as usual. She did not give up because she had to make them listen. Then she remembered a street preacher in Sangre Grande having a loud device. She went to the town of Sangre Grande and looked for him. He told her where the music shop was in Sangre Grande. There she purchased her own bullhorn. She would lock up her stall an hour a day to give her message. She would say often "All these trees will rot; you will not be able to replant them again. Snow you will eat to hurt your teeth and not food to warm your belly. The sun here will be blocked out. Matelot will freeze first then the storm would spread across the Earth with unbridled magnitude. Leave here friends and neighbors! Go up the Caribbean! Go Venezuela! Give yourself more time to escape. Get a sweater and winter jacket! Always keep them nearby. Prepare for the winter storm comin. wha comin is not the snow you would love to hear crunch under yuh foot, or snow to play snowball fights with. This coldness would reach through your flesh and freeze your blood and bones. If it doesn't kill you in the night you will still wake with dead feet and lifeless grey fingers. When this winter freezes the ground, your legs will turn to ice axes and anchor yuh curled up, mummified corpse forever. When this wind howls you will pull the scarf tightly over your whole face and bend yuh head in terror. The wind would laugh and rejoice as it froze armies and infants alike. You would not find the strength to open your mouth to curse the blizzard. It would be colder than any minus thirty degrees winter night in Nizhny Tagil. It go be cold enough to flash freeze all life." People passing her would often spit out a heated retort. The woman selling peppers and fresh seasonings had told her "Shut yuh mouth! Is you who is d blight. You ha all d jumbie here! Tha is why d place getting so cold!" The villagers believed in human barometers. However it would be daft for them to have believed Ma Ethelrida's manure; that Matelot will be the origin of a giant snow storm soon. A man who taught physics at a school in Toco-the near by town, had chastised people for listening to Ma Ethelrida "doh let she fool yuh! De Earth is always coldest at de poles. Always! That will never change. How d hell snow going to spread from d equator? She doh even have one degree in nutting." But they all feared Ma Ethelrida more than any storm; because they thought she had powers through black arts.

David would hear her predictions often, while parked at the unofficial taxi stand. Before her prophesies David had never really thought about snow; except when he heard Christmas carols on the radio. But when he first heard her preaching outside the church, the coldness had crept into Matelot, and he dreamt of snow ad nauseam.

When David was around ten years old, he and other mischievous children, after school was over, would routinely tease Ma Ethelrida as if she were a witch. They would stay at the edge of her yard and shriek at the top of their lungs "soucouyant! soucouyant!" and run away; which in Trinidad is a type of bloodsucking hag. At night David and all the school children avoided her house because of the mendacious propaganda; that she was a female demon. Everyone told scary stories about her when he was a schoolboy. At that young age when David saw a dark corner in his house, he would be certain Ma Ethelrida was lurking in the blackness. His fear would compel him to look at the faded picture of the risen Jesus, his father hung over their front door, for comfort. Despite their fears when her fruits were ripe, straining the branches and dangling low, and they were sure Ma Ethelrida was inside her house, David and his school friends would sneak into her yard to steal her fruits. She had two soursop trees, a sapodilla, a five finger, several mango trees, coconut, plum, cashew and vangueria madagascariensis- locally called Chinee tambrand. The children swore she had the sweetest fruits because she made a deal with the devil.

Ma Ethelrida never travelled with David when he just started working taxi. He would toot his horn at her or gesture wildly with his hand to no avail. She had marked him as one of the boys who liked to tease her; even though he was grown up and reformed now. In those days she would only ever ride in one taxi, which was driven by Mr. Harry. Ma Ethelrida met Mr. Harry through going to Sangre Grande weekly; where she would purchase in bulk raw materials to make her soaps and healing medicines. They met in front of garish shop signs, on a crammed taxi stand, alongside a smelly rat-infested box drain, during a stifling heat wave one Friday. Ma Ethelrida had been waiting in another taxi with greasy, sticky, maroon coloured leather seats. She heard that normally quiet taxi driver sob suddenly. He turned around and the anguish contorting his face made Ma Ethelrida gasp in horror. He was sucking tears and snot into his trembling mouth. Then he attempted to wipe his long tears and recomposes himself. The poor man blurted out "I can't carry yuh again! My son gay. My son gay! So, I cryin." Ma Etelridad stared back with her mouth open not knowing what to do or say. Eventually the man stopped crying and got out of the car. He called breathlessly to the taxi behind him "Hareee! Hareee! Spanish! Come! Take this woman. She goin Matelot with she bags." Harry replied "What troubling you so boi? Rum in your arse awat?"

"eeeee eeeee My son is a homo. Eeeee eeeee!" the man cried unable to hide his utter disappointment."

"Doh take that on boi. Doh study that! De times different now," Harry tried to console with both hands on his waist looking very concerned for his fellow driver.

"I can't. eeeee eeeee!" Harry knew the man would go home with a bottle of rum to try to drown his sorrows. Harry sadly turned away and took Ma Ethelrida's goods to pack it in his trunk. She got into the front seat of Harry's taxi and they drove off in silence. Two minutes into the drive Harry uttered a mocking "eeeee eeeee!", pretending to wipe his eyes of tears. Then Ma Ethelrida burst into cackle.

"Oh gosh like yuh mocking d man, ah what?" He had to pull the car aside and then brayed with laughter. They both carried on until their stomachs hurt.

"Ent yuh know mister more and more people comin out now? The guavament will give them equal rights, but they will want to teach that way in schools which I don't like."

"I understand but call me Harry or Spanish if you want." Harry stated cordially. From then on, she would always travel with Harry. Mr. Harry was from Toco; the town between Sangre Grande and Matelot. He was a handsome man of Spanish descent in his late fifties. Ma Ethelrida never dabbed makeup on her face, but she would use minimal lipstick and face powder whenever she hired Mr. Harry. The howling phantom winter winds that she heard, that would scare her daily, would go silent as his sun and moonlight beamed into her cold veins. Mr. Harry knew exactly how she would sit in his taxi. She would be in a straight posture with her both hands holding shut the top of her purse, which she kept on her lap. He would clean and perfume his car anytime he knew he had to pick her up. She would ask him how he was. He would gently pat her hand and say he was doing well. She would give him a beaming smile and her eyes would lock tenderly to his. Then he would almost forget to drive off. When Ma Ethelrida got attacked and beaten by the church cleaner, named Cherry-Ann, she had called Harry. When Harry saw her with her arm in a homemade sling it almost made him cry. He carried her to get an x-ray of her arm, luckily it was not fractured. When he dropped her back to her home, he hugged her gently. He had barely felt the caress, what he felt more was the pain of letting her go. That day Harry finally got Ma Ethelrida to stop giving him a taxi fare. He wanted to help her and to be with her often.

Ma Ethelrida found out later that someone had paid that woman to scare her into shutting up. But the thing that almost made her leave the village forever was not the fear of being harmed by paid thugs, but by promise that Harry made. Harry looked deeply into her eyes and swore that if she lived with him, she would be his sun, moon and sky. It hurt worst than death to stay in Matelot, but she bit back the pain; her purpose for being born was to stop the icy doom coming. Despite all her troubles Harry wanted to still give her little moments of happiness. Harry had booked a guest house in Tobago for the long weekend for them both. He wanted it to be a thrilling surprise to Ma Ethelrida that would raise her spirits. He knew she had never left Trinidad before. Harry was falling in love with her and her with him.

Before they got to go on the trip Mr. Harry died suddenly right inside his taxi. In the taxi stand, while waiting to carry Ma Ethelrida to his house in Toco, Mr. Harry had suffered a massive heart attack. Ma Ethelrida had collapsed on the road when she saw him being loaded into the ambulance. David saw she was laying face first on the dusty road too weak to crawl to the side. No one was going to help her they believed she was cursed. David felt compassion for her and scrambled out of his taxi to get her. He lifted her into his taxi. He knew exactly where she lived and brought her to her home. He realized that day how vulnerable she was and what all the lies told had done to her. From that day he chose to be her friend. David could only guest what she must have lost. David would often visit at her stall when she started back to sell her herbal soaps and healing concoctions. The first stall Ma Ethelrida had was painted in a sacred dark green with magical symbols of stars, ringed planets and light rays. That wooden structure was burned down and the arsonist was never found out. He helped her rebuild a humble little shop, trying to redeem himself for the way he had menaced this wise lady when he was young. Gradually Ma Ethelrida made him into the survivalist he had become. She thought him about eating right, secret brotherhood conspiracies, alternative histories, medicines and meditation- to deal with mental stresses. She taught David that man lived in a materialistic age, which was part of a cycle. And that some ages end in cataclysm. The period they lived in certainly was not enlightened, since people were oblivious to the malignant cold coming. David now felt like her adopted son and loved her as his mother. He told her "I now realize that you truly saw what others couldn't see. You see the world beyond the physical." She taught David that he had senses that he was commonly aware of, and then he had some rare ones that he didn't access often enough. Ma Ethelrida explained to him, "David the rare powers you have are the prophetic dreams, premonitions, the familiarity of new places or situations, and that moment when you make peace with yuh unconscious mind by letting it speak." She had long found her rare senses and they grew more powerful with each day. She dreamt of the day when this great task would be over. David would stay here with her and fight; the world needed them. It was their destiny to stop the coming apocalypse. It seemed only they were awakened to it; the rest of the world would not spare a thought for Matelot. Ma Ethelrida taught David what to wear, how to layer clothing to regulate body temperature, how to limit sweating, and where the best place to stay warm was. She got some winter clothes for him from the US. He now had at home and in his van some knitted Angola wool sweaters. He saved his money and bought a digital SLR camera. He and Ma Ethelrida needed the high resolution, telephoto and low light capabilities of this type of camera. They took furtive pictures of the cult group there, to discover their whole membership and activities. Now the camera was in the enemy's hands, with all the photos David took of the cult recently.

When David reached Ma Ethelrida, he cried out hysterically "Ma I can't see! I can't see so good! Ma!"

The shrill cry pierced the still evening. Ma Ethelrida ran out of the kitchen where she was making roti for their dinner. She yanked her heavy coat tearing it off the hook on the front door. The cold air outside smacked her face. She ran down the little steps as fast as her numbed joints would allow to help David. She put an arm around his waist and helped him inside. She guided David to sit by the still warm tawah. Ma Ethelrida made hot cocoa tea for them in a big enamel cup. They ate sada roti and zaboca choka.

"Boi yuh still seeing stars?"

"We have to do something Ma. I will not flinch! We will set the roof of the church on fire and chase them out!" She had a small neat bundle of dried bush crisscrossed up in brown twine, which she placed on some glowing coals inside her black hawan pot. The surreal vapor made David's aches and fears float away quickly.

"If only we had more help boi. It have Sherlyn father who is trying to come up, but he aged like me."

Uncle Bob

U ncle Bob felt that he had a tenacious subconscious link with his missing daughter, Sherlyn. Daily her voice pleaded for redemption.

She's alive, she must be, she's out there still, I know. Twenty years is a long eternity without mih daughter. She missing.so long. I want to search for her again in Matelot. She begged me in my dreams 'daddy come and look for me.' She talks about ice in Matelot. I know soon it would be possible to see her again. Uncle Bob mind was always reeling with thoughts of Matelot. He was the only one battling to find his daughter; everyone else had long stopped caring. Uncle Bob sat before dawn waiting for his niece, Donna to come. He remembered Donna was always an intelligent child, and now a kind woman. She had long beautiful hair and flawless skin. Donna and her husband would sometimes come for fruits. Uncle Bob had downs (jujube), orange, avocado, lime and mangoes. Her husband was much older than her and had medical complications. He thought maybe she had the heart and instinct to help him get to Matelot, to find Sherlyn. He knew the drive would be long for Donna, but they would find the place together. If he forgot the way to Matelot, he knew Sherlyn's beacon would guide him.

Thank God Mary is not coming with me. He would ask Donna as soon as the car was moving away from his wife, Mary. Marry had arranged for Donna to carry him to the mental hospital. Mary had arranged the counseling session with the psychologist. She was not the same woman he had married. This other Mary talked on the phone to her cult leader daily. It was the cult leader's orders that he be taken to a certain Dr. William. Uncle Bob had heard that when he picked up the extension phone to eavesdrop on his wife's conversation. Mary would often begin and end her secret phone conversations repeating the phrase "Light and Ice!" He did not trust hospitals though and would have to be dragged along. He knew if he started taking pills it would fog up his mind, and Sherlyn would be lost. They would give him pills for anxiety, depression, and to sleep. The pills would certainly be too toxic to him. He was haunted every day since reading an eerie article about Matelot, a year and some months ago. It roused him out of inaction. He had found in the daily newspapers a short opinion piece written by Sherlyn's mother-in-law, Ma Ethelrida. Sherlyn's mother-in-law was featured in the newspapers as the 'village witch'. She said in the article that the land was dying of an unnatural frost; which was emptying her village of its residents. Seeing Ma Ethelrida's name, who he once blamed for his daughter's death, brought on a feeling that he couldn't recover from. While all leads to his missing daughter had gone cold where he was, Ma Ethelrida could breathe life back into his search. He wondered if Ma Ethelrida found her son Big Jim, who went missing around the same time as Sherlyn.

The rising sun of the new day blasted the mountains with pure rays, but the light could not dispel the persistent shadow on him. These days' dawn and dusk were all meaningless. He felt trapped in San Juan; so far from where he lost his daughter. Loneliness pressed on him. Two nights ago, he got himself into trouble; where his wife questioned his sanity. The electrical power in the area had been out at that time. However, the place was brightly lit because it was the night before the full moon. That night had and uneasy, eerie, silence to it. He couldn't sleep thinking about Sherlyn, so he sat in the porch looking out. A droning sound reached his ears that he recognized as his Hillman avenger's engine. He fought with all his will not to hear his car idling perfectly, but he knew that engine sound. He had modified the twin-carburetor engine himself so many years ago. The sound had to be white noise from a nearby generator or something, or else it had to be a figment of his imagination. As he looked at his avenger, the car had a beautiful pearlescent paintjob. The tattered tarpaulin, with all the rust and molds, which covered it, was gone. The glass was crystal clear again and not opaque with dust. Through the car window he could see his daughter. She was a young child version of herself. She was behind the steering wheel white as snow sitting looking directly at him. Her eyes were black orbs scrubbed by a violent blizzard. They were like two forbidden holes spewing strange radiation in the depths of space. Then her lips quickly became blue, and then she stifled. He ran to help her despite his fear. The apparition blurred and grayed in his consciousness until he fell and passed out. All he could remember after was his wife and daughter dragging him out of the car. When they locked him in his room he had scraped on his wall, using his screwdriver "did malice made the ice grow? Did her grief make the cold wind blow? A spell cast on a wicked day work to curse the brine of Matelot bay." Uncle Bob felt helpless in this prison his home had become. He felt his wife's forceful will, ever-present to crush his resolve. It was only locked away in his room that he really acknowledged to himself, his pitiful state. When the alarm rang in the next room, it dawned on him that this would be his last chance to run. "I will die if I can't run." He lamented.

This morning he had yanked out his loaded pistol from its hiding place and stuffed it in his roomy jacket pocket. Uncle Bob indefatigably thought about his long-missing daughter Sherlyn, long-deceased to everyone else. Thinking about Sherlyn became a nervous disorder that kept him from sleeping. He would not take sleep brought on artificially by nasty smelling pills.

In his thirties he had the best electronic shop in his area. He was even sponsored a trip to Holland by the electronic brand he sold. But his unwillingness at the time to migrate the newer semi-conductor technology- which had a relentless pace- left him way behind in the field of electronic devices. He was too obstinate to abandon his vacuum tube electronics. At 64 he could still remember how to troubleshoot any piece of equipment that used vacuum tubes for amplification of signals or delivering power. He thought his mind was still agile. However, his wife was always telling him he was senile- unable to do even trivial, day to day things. She wanted him to just sit and read his prayer book; until his eyes fell out their sockets. His wife Mary was two years younger than him but that didn't give her the right to call him an old fool. She had an off-putting personality over the last few years, especially since she was deeper in her false religion. After joining the secret church, she took control of their relationship. Mary had an authoritative way of speaking with many veiled treats.

Before Sherlyn disappeared all, he was concerned with was being best brand salesman. He had many regrets now. In recent years he should have been paying more attention to how his freedoms were being taken away by Mary. Unfortunately broken by grief, he was just as eager to be the slave, as she was eager to be the master. Her devout catholic stance on life that attracted him at first was gone forever. He knew her belief had become inauthentic; since she was really just a secret cult acolyte. He didn't believe she would let him divorce. She was a robot programmed by this cult to destroy his life.

"She would never let me leave her." the romance-

what little there was- in the marriage was long gone, none of them could say or dared remember what the romantic attraction at the beginning of the marriage was. Uncle Bob had five children with Mary. Her favorite was her eldest son. He chose banking as a career instead of following in his father's footsteps. All her children except Sherlyn had migrated to North America. Sherlyn had a delicate nose like her mother but had her father's wavy brown hair, and his catlike eyes. It was Mary who had forced Sherlyn to marry so early. Sherlyn was annoyed that her mother had made Big Jim agree to a wedding. That was on the first occasion that she had brought Big Jim home. She feared that if they continued in secret, she would get caught with him, and Mary would blow the whole thing out of proportion. At the table alone with him she stated that he may not be able to see Sherlyn again if his intention was not to marry Sherlyn soon. So before leaving Big Jim agreed to a wedding day not far off. Uncle Bob was disappointed because he knew the marriage was pushed only because of his wife's paranoia; that Sherlyn would get pregnant and bring shame to her. Sherlyn's life went too fast after she brought Big Jim home. She wasn't ready for that type of commitment; she just liked the novel attention she was getting. But she had need for concern sometimes she could sense a dark, underlying possessiveness in Big Jim. She hoped he could control his anger. She wondered if she would be hit during a jealous fit from him. Matelot was a remote village away from her family and friends and it was difficult for her to adjust to life there with her husband big Jim. She lived there the last two years of her life. Uncle Bob lost touch with his daughter after she left San Juan to go and live with her husband. Uncle Bob wondered about the type of women he might have found if he had separated from Mary. It would certainly make sense to leave Mary if he could; despite him finding a good match or not.

After reading the article by Ma Ethelrida he had secretly written to her; unknown to his wife. Ma Ethelrida was given Uncle's Bob number in his letter to her. They contacted each other secretly on the phone from then. By some means, after all these years, he had to find his way back to Matelot village because his daughter was haunting him, pleading in his head for help. He was certain he and Ma Ethelrida could find Sherlyn. He stood a good chance of reaching Matelot if he could get away from his sinister wife.

Twenty Years Ago

*B*ig *Jim was twenty-four years old. He was six feet two inches tall and weighed three hundred and ten pounds. He was a very muscular except for his huge belly. From his teenage years Big Jim was feared by most men in the village, because of his temper. He was a mixed-race Trinidadian with brown skin. He was raised by his mother alone as his father died when he was a baby. When he was a boy, he liked to imitate the moves of his wrestling heroes; but any other boys in the village that played wrestling with him would get seriously injured, from a broken bone or a cracked skull. Ma Ethelrida always had to fight vicious parents who came to avenge their bruised and battered children. One good quality Big Jim had was that as he became a man, he protected his mother; no one would dare to harm his mother. Big Jim's first job, at eighteen, was as a security guard; but he was fired for using excessive force on an intruder. And then Big Jim got a permanent job working with the government. He was the bus driver for the Toco to Sangre Grande route, and being given a* *bad drive had crashed the bus he drove. He was convinced someone was working obeah on him. He thought one of his neighbors was burning kakajab for him in their fire. He was convinced their hands were 'dirty'. He bought a nine-inch votive candle- with a saint on it, and an eight-ounce bottle of holy water. He then came home early from work. He said the our father prayer and lit his candle. His wife Sherlyn was then twenty years old, and she had her one-year old baby boy in her arms. When He sat on that couch holding his chest, telling Sherlyn what had happened. Ma Ethelrida was in the kitchen listening. Somehow Sherlyn chose that time to reveal to Big Jim about her affair. She loved another man. She spoke it out hoarsely in spurts. She told Big Jim that she had a friend on the beach called Jokull. She started to sob. Ma Ethelrida's blood had run cold. She knew Big Jim had a bad temper, so she went to shield Sherlyn in her arms. The baby boy, Jude, started to cry loudly. Big Jim only then suspected that the baby was not his but Jokull's. Jokull was the tall European man with long golden Rasta hair. He stayed in the church sometimes, but mostly he lived in the shack by the beach. He slammed his hand down on the table three times, violently splintering the little wooden coffee table. Everyone stiffened at the blows he gave to the table.*

"Alyuh playing de ass with me now? Alyuh playing with my head! He turned to sherlyn she shrieked and clutched the baby frozen with fear. She saw murder in his bulging eyes and his sullen face. Ma Ethelrida could see that the sacred candle and water did not help her son. It was as

if some entity was in him now and this demon stole his huge body to rage.

"You have ah man? You have ah man? He bellowed repeatedly. Ma Ethelrida intervened bravely "who is she man? Who is she man?" She was trying to stall Big Jim, but she knew very well who Sherlyn's lover was. Ma Ethelrida pleaded with her son that it was a mistake, and that Sherlyn was naïve. She begged him earnestly not to do anything. He barely heard his mother with the rage that was shaking him. She told Sherlyn to hide with the baby. Big Jim was lost to himself; he was in a world of anguish. He roughly sharpened up a machete; they used to cut up coconuts with, and he left in a zombie like state. He walked down to Jokull's shack, which was just past the fishing sheds on the beach. Big Jim screamed Jokull's name, but there was no answer. He only woke Jokull from his slumber. Big Jim found a gas can in one of the pirogues anchored on the beach. Corbeaux scattered taking to the air over the shack. Jokull spied Big Jim coming down the beach through a peep hole in his shack. Jokull became terrified and jumped through his back window. He climbed up the cliff towards the church. Big Jim found his door open and stormed in. He doused petrol in Jokull's shack. He turned over the little bed and found a cardboard box of letters his wife had wrote to Jokull. He read that they had a secret place they would go to, in a boat Jokull had access to. They would climb up on an iceberg, pass through a cave in it, and then come out in a foreign land. They would frolic there and make love. They had plans to live there one day soon with their son Jude. He sat on the ground in the stench of the gasoline

crying. He screamed and growled, and maniacally knocked over things. He turned the bed right so he could lie on it and he lit himself on the bed; wishing Sherlyn was under him to burn up. He did not feel the heat of the fire he only dreamed of the iceberg Jokull and Sherlyn had written about. The flames quickly gobbled up the little ply-board shack. When Ma Ethelrida reached the fire the villagers and the parish priest were already there. They had doused the fire out, but in the ash Big Jim remains were not found. People had seen Jokull running to the church. They had seen Big Jim go in Jokull's shack for sure and wondered where he had disappeared to. Jokull had run breathlessly to Brother Aquilo. Brother Aquilo oversaw protecting, monitoring and travelling with Jokull. Ivar was Brother Aquilo's underling. Their cover was as visiting lay persons in the Catholic Church there in Matelot. They had spent over a year in Matelot as guests of the church. The religious order they belonged to had made a substantial financial contribution to the church.

"Help me! Help! Help! Big Jim is coming to kill me! Please hide me!" Jokull cried. Brother Aquilo quickly organized a room in the church for Jokull to hide, from Big Jim. Jokull was watched in Matelot since the day he came here. Brother Aquilo knew that Jokull was having sex with Sheryn for over a year. But he never told his leaders about Jokull and the woman. Brother Aquilo didn't think Jokull was the chosen one. Brother Aquilo felt like he was sent on a vacation there in Matelot. He didn't want to waste his time watching Jokull; another, Light and Ice Church, desultory experiment. He just made up false reports on Jokull for

main membership to swallow. He enjoyed hearing the ocean waves; he enjoyed the warm water, and blue Caribbean sky. "No way could that lame, inbred introvert Jokull be the savior of my Order." Brother Aquilo knew Big Jim and his reputation. Brother Aquilo heard the story of someone who had stolen from Ma Ethelrida's yard. The thief was just standing outside the shop by the church when Big Jim walked up to him. Big Jim had a pillowcase in his hand. Big Jim said to the man that he would just give him just one brief warning. Before the man could respond to him Big Jim made the man scream in pain, as he shattered some of the man's bones. The pillowcase had about eight medium pad locks and some river stones in it. When the pillowcase had ripped, and the locks and stones flung out into the shop breaking a glass showcase, then Big Jim let the shop owner help the bleeding man. Brother Aquilo should have known that there would be trouble. The Order would call him and Jokull back for reprogramming; or to be tortured and killed. Jokull had warned Sherlyn not to tell Big Jim, but that was not enough. She would not listen, and he didn't know when she was going to tell her berserk hubby.

"Jokull tell me did you see the iceberg? You must tell us if you see the iceberg?" Brother Aquilo probed.

"No. No!" Jokull would never tell them about his secret place. He and Sherlyn would go there now as soon as they could get away from Big Jim and the Order. Jokull many times begged Sherlyn to stay in the foreign land they had found, but she told him she made vows and wanted to leave with a clear conscience. She always chickened out from telling Big Jim because of his dreadful temper.

"You will have to leave here for a while. We cannot allow you to get killed, you belong to us. We let you live so you can find the ice here for us. You have failed us falling for that married woman. What did you expect to leave the order for her? They won't allow any of us to betray the order unscathed. Remember that we could put you in the ice room. Don't bite the hand that lets you live." Brother Aquilo admonished.

"You can't threaten me Brother Aquilo. The ice room is far from here!" Jokull said bravely. *This was a disaster for Brother Aquilo. He would have to inject Jokull to make him pass out.*

"What about my son?" Jokull pleaded.

"I knew she had your baby and not Big Jim's. Yes of course he has to go! What's yours is ours," Brother Aquilo answered. *He called his subordinate Ivar who had the tranquilizer for Jokull. Brother Aquilo did not want to leave Matelot to be tortured. He had to make his escape before the other members forced him to return back to the Light and Ice Church headquarters in Norway. He heard the news that the old leader of the order had died. He knew the new leader the counsel had chosen was sadistic, and a product of inbreeding who would show him no mercy. He decided he would head to Venezuela, by boat and never return. Ivar's job was to watch Brother Aquilo to make sure he was not derelict in his duty. Ivar's secret order was to get Jokull, his son Jude, Sherlyn and Brother Aquilo back to Light and Ice Church in Norway.*

Ma Ethelrida went back to her home to search for Sherlyn and Big Jim; along with a policewoman, who give up early and told her to contact the station whenever either one turned up. Some people came to keep up a wake for her son, but she left them, she hoped Big Jim was alive still. She could not believe what her son did. She had always prayed for her family. She thought maybe if his father was around, he would be a different man; but his father died when he was a boy. She wondered what part of Big Jim's love had all this murderous hate in it. She searched for Sherlyn until it was almost dawn. The last place she searched was the old, abandoned catholic grounds. She found her leaning against a headless, vine overrun statue of the Virgin. She had looked crazed; she was bitten all over by mosquito and cut by the razor grass. Ma Ethelrida picked up the baby and helped Sherlyn to stand. They went limping home together. Sherlyn asked "what did Big Jim do? Did he hurt Jokull?"

"I don't know where they are," Ma Ethelrida said with fear in her eyes.

"I'm sorry for all of this," Sherlyn barely managed to say.

Ma Ethelrida could not console Sherlyn. She had a few sips of coffee, but Sherlyn never touched hers. Then Ma Ethelrida carried her to church. She had carried Sherlyn to the church; hoping that the goodly priest there could do something. She did not know the nefarious people present in the church she was leading Sherlyn to. They were contravening the rules of the church. They had made the priest miss mass today. The old priest there was the only thing standing in their way. Sherlyn seemed so inconsolable. Sunday service was going on, so they had to wait until it was over to get counseling. Sherllyn said she wanted to see Jokull as they sat in the back bench of the church. At times Ma Ethelrida felt like she did not know the girl at all. Sherlyn told her that she and her friend Jokull had been to an iceberg located out at sea. It sounded like madness what she said,

"Me and Jokull saw an iceberg. He took me too it sometimes when he borrowed a boat. There is still something not far out there in the sea. Do you believe me?" Her last hour in the church was a febrile struggle to keep in touch with reality. Ma Ethelrida sat in the church anxiously waiting for the service to end. There were visiting members of a local catholic charismatic group holding the mass. She was looking for Brother Aquilo among the people there as the parish priest was not there. She would ask him if he knew where Jokull was. She thought maybe he could also help Sherlyn. While Ivar and his minions were spellbinding the people who came to church, Brother Aquilo was freeing Jokull. He told Jokull to take the boat to the Matelot River and get his son from Ma Ethelrida.

"Tonight, I would meet you and Jude by the boat and we would leave for Venezuela." Jokull nodded in agreement to Brother Aquilo's plan. The first week Brother Aquilo was there in Matelot he had reached out to Ma Ethelrida, after church. He was interested in her because people there said she was a witch and cursed. He was a strange man to Ma Ethelrida, with his own charms, but she did not see any duplicity in him. He told Ma Ethelrida if he could live his life again, he would not join the religious order he did. When they had the opportunity to converse, he would

ask her what she dreamt and if she glimpsed any strange ice there. He feared that he had become a skeptic and wanted Ma Ethelrida to confirm that the place really had power and magic. She remembered the local charismatic group that Brother Aquilo came with last year. It seemed odd to her now that a man like Brother Aquilo would come with them. They had descended on the naive village, with their judgmental sermons about the villager's false gods in Matelot. They fanatically wanted to mark everyone with the blood of the lamb. Ma Ethelrida had an aversion for the charismatic Catholics because they seemed a bit pushy. She was suspicious of the waving of hands in the air, and the loud clapping, and other ostentatious antics; which she found was out of place with the quite beauty of the church. She was not a staunch catholic, present at the mass at the church every Sunday, but she believed in having more quietude and humility in the house of God. They- the charismatic members, would call her idea of church a 'dead church'. They had come to revive the church by making it a circus in her opinion.

Sherlyn had seemed irritated by the fiery clapping and frenzied tambourines of the young charismatic people, they made snake-like sounds to her. They had all the church goers under some paralyzing spell. Sherlyn suddenly shot up from her seat and stood rigid. Ma Ethelrida grabbed her hand and coaxed her to sit down but her mind was somewhere else. She should have carried her outside away from the punishment of that noisy mass. Something attacked her subconscious mind. Vibrations sent from the cult group in the church drove her into hysterics. Her face became contorted and wild. Her beautiful eyes were lost forever. Her lips vibrated and turned into a snarl. Ma Ethelrida sat paralyzed with shock as Sherlyn ran snarling straight at the young singer behind the podium. The not ordained man outstretched his hand cupping her face and stopped her in mid run. She fell backward mercifully on the long wooden bench and not on the terrazzo floor. Cult members in the front row were now choking her. She clawed into the air. The tight pressure of unwanted hands around her neck and limbs made her faint. They wanted to kill her right there in the church. Her skin was cold and clammy after Brother Aquilo wrestled their violent hands away. Ma Ethelrida winched in tears because she had already been through so much. She was a nice girl and she loved her. Sherlyn opened her eyes and got upright, and then she broke into a run; screaming out of the church. Ma Ethelrida was praying in a in a state of semi-suffocation.

"St. Michael the archangel defends us…" she ran for and hugged Sherlyn's crying baby tightly Sherlyn had to run for her life. While Brother Aquilo watched Sherlyn flee Ivar snuck up to him and injected him with a tranquilizer. Brother Aquilo fell down and the members carried him away.

Fear, shame, and confusion propelled Sherlyn's feet, as they ran franticly to the sea. In the water she scrambled into a pirogue that was being untied by a group of fishermen. She gained control of the engine throttle as the men froze in surprise. Two of the men fell off the boat as she revved the boat. It rocked and swerved hard as it shot off. The men cursed and screamed with their hands in the air.

The boat tossed up in the air and then it was gone. The ocean was a better way to escape for her. Sherlyn would have stopped at Salybia Bay and tried to get a maxi back to San Juan. Instead she met with an accident slamming the pirogue into a wall of floating ice. There was no time to slow down or even turn hard to avoid it. She wouldn't have minded death then, she wanted demise. She was especially distraught about causing so much trouble for son. When the pirogue hit the ice instead of meeting a tragic end by drowning or breaking her neck, on impact, this ice captured her body- but without damage to her bones, or pressure to stop her breathing. This ice became her prison. There was no passage out to a foreign land like she and Jokull had used before. It seemed to her that only Jokull wielded that power; to make the iceberg a portal. The iceberg, above water, was basically two big domes connected by a bridge. She was in an upright prism in one of the domes. There were nine wolf men there with her; in nine tall prisms. It looked like nine copies of the same man, all with differing personalities; one was snarling, another was laughing maniacally, yet another was just menacingly steering at her. In no time she realized with horror it was Big Jim, he was now split into different monsters. They could not talk to her through their prism glass, but she saw their hate towards her. Jokull had a special gift to see the iceberg entity and through his fear had sent Big Jim, here first, to the iceberg reality. Then Big Jim through his anger used the energy of the iceberg to trap Sherlyn. But as much as he projected himself out of his prison cell, he couldn't touch her physically. From her alcove she saw that she and the Big Jim wolves were in one cavern, and it was connected by a narrow tube, to another cavern, of similar big size. The whole place was composed of a wavy surfaced ice, and it had an ethereal blue glow. She could clearly hear the water splashing outside, and when pieces of the iceberg broke off occasionally. She was in the part of the iceberg above the water. Below here feet she suspected there would be more caverns with more prisoners.

She wanted to live to tell about this iceberg. At times she thought she was dreaming in a hospital somewhere, drugged heavily with potent medicines. Or she thought she had finally lost her mind from brain trauma. She wished sometimes she could wake up in the ocean threading water free from her prison. The substance around her only looked like ice but was an unknown entity - some metaphysical material, or a separate reality beyond the dimensions that men know.

The Appointment

In the dark Donna's hand flopped around her head, like a fish on sand, to take off the relentless alarm on her bed head. Her husband Ted did not stir from the thick depths of his sleep. She got up and felt her way about the edge of the bed while stumbling out of the dark bedroom. She knocked cold numb knuckles on her daughter's door and called hoarsely to wake her. Sophia was her teenage daughter. Sophia awoke but did not answer. Two days ago, her mother yelled at her and slapped her around. Her mother had never hit her like that before. Sophia had stolen money from Donna, and she got found out. They were not talking to each other since then. If Donna wanted something from Sophia, Ted her father, would relay the messages for them. Sophia was fifteen years old. She was taller than her mother and lanky. It seems to Donna like Sophia even hated to even stand sometimes and would rather lie down all day and listen to music. Sophia liked to play the same album over and over all week. She liked to scribble her favorite lyrics on a little blue company diary her father gave her. Donna had already forgiven Sophia and just wanted things to be normal again.

"Just now mom!", finally came a voice from behind the door.

Donna was worried for her uncle bob, which she had to get to the St. Ann's hospital, this morning. Her aunt Mary had asked her to do this favor on the phone two days ago. She would have to drop Sophia to school afterwards. Donna hoped her aunt was wrong about uncle bob. She hoped that there was some exaggeration in her aunt's account of Uncle Bob. Donna had not seen him, face to face, for some months, although she lived not far away by car. She had a childhood flash back of Uncle Bob handing out sweets to her and her little brother. He was dressed in his white short-sleeve shirt and black tie, with his pen neatly clipped in his shirt pocket. Whenever he stopped by in those days, he would always have sweets in his pants pockets for them. She remembered his deep smile lines would run from his clever grey eyes to under his chin. He always looked perceptive in his raffia fedora hat. She wiped a small tear from the corners of her eyes. She poked into the refrigerator to pluck out bottled water for herself and Sophia. Sophia grabbed her mobile phone which had her melancholic gothic treasure throve of music and stuffed it in her pocket. Donna spun a couple of times in front the mirror making brisk minor adjustments to her clothes and hair. She kissed her sleeping spouse on his cheek to say goodbye. They got in the car and headed for Uncle Bob that lived less than a mile away.

She told Sophia what her aunt said on the phone that he was not himself lately. Late in the night last week he had sneaked outside, on the grass where his car stayed-derelict and rotting. He pulled off the dingy, mildewed tarpaulin removing the stone weights holding it in place like he was possessed. His crumbling car hadn't been started for years, and the battery was removed. It would take a talented, patient mechanic to ever get the car started again.

"Betty and aunty were shocked to find their front door wide open and breeze blowing the curtains in the middle of the night. They thought a burglar was in the house, or that someone was trying to steal Uncle Bob's car. Betty came downstairs with a loaded shot gun and almost shot him; her own father. He was in the car where he kept turning the key trying to start the engine. He had started crying loudly in the car. This naturally made them scared. She went to their family physician who suspected a nervous disorder that needed to be checked out. So, Aunt Mary made an appointment for today. They said he screamed at times and ranted about ice freezing over Matelot." Donna told Sophia.

Donna always looked at the statue of the Amerindian as she drove past it on the Old Road. It was brought centuries ago by Spanish colonizers of the island. On top a tall, cylindrical structure that held a winding staircase stood the proud Amerindian man looking to the horizon. Donna's father had said he ran up and down the steps in the staircase when he was a child. This Amerindian's history was now mired in legend. The legend she heard was that he warned the Spaniards, about an ambush by his people, and so saved the invaders. Wondering about the history of this land, along the banks of the San Juan River, was a distraction for the state she would find her uncle in. She even called San Juan by the original Amerindian name Aricagua. The indigenous people here did not worship Aries, the Greek god of war, or the Hebrew Yahweh, they had their own cemies. They were victims of a great genocide that wiped out millions of aborigine people. Men, from across the Atlantic, came for low hanging fruits from the islands of the Caribbean, and the continent of America. They were men who believed that giant sea monsters would swallow their ships but risked their lives for new lands and gold. The Aborigines thought they could trade equally with the more sophisticated people but were conquered. It was a ritual on the Earth with a great negative energy pattern upon mankind. It turned men into cattle with enslaving systems. In 1498 admiral Columbus came upon Trinidad in la nao. He stopped for water because he had a low supply. His men took water from a brook at Erin bay- where they found footprints of men already there. He did not expect much gold and continued to the mainland of Venezuela. The empire he served would not set up their systems in Trinidad until decades later. Before Columbus there was already trade among the indigenous people, between Trinidad (Iere) and the mainland. Just by his men setting their foot, on the islands here, he claimed the Amerindians and their land for European royals, thousands of miles away, and for his bankers. Over the centuries trade was set up for first gold, then food, and today oil and cocaine.

When she reached, they were all dressed and ready waiting in the porch. Uncle Bob climbed tiredly into the car. Mary looked acerbic as ever as she got in the back seat with her husband. Uncle Bob wondered if she would ever understand that their life was a lie. The only thing real to him was to get to Matelot. Uncle Bob turned away from her with an annoyed expression on his weathered face. A stray dog cried eerily as uncle bob left his front gate in his niece's car. Sophia was surprised that Mary talked so freely to her as they drove along the Old road Mary asked her if she knew about the explosion that happened in the sky. "Yuh don't watch news girl. They say the end of the Earth commin. And d bible really say these are the last days. Yuh must read d bible girl." They passed Pamberi steel pan theater and then the San Juan cemetery- where most of their relatives were buried. Donna remembered last carnival hearing Pamberi play the local music on there steel drum instruments, at the Queen's Park Savannah.

Donna parked outside the church fence below the shady poui tree, with some fat bumble bees flirting around. The church yard was empty and she could see the Marian grotto. The statue of the virgin always reminded her about the miracle she saw on the local news, at Mejagori. Missionaries from Spain had built the church and named the town after San Juan Baptista.

Uncle Bob thought about opening the car and just quickly walking away. He had enough money stashed in his pocket to reach Matelot. Uncle Bob grimaced as he looked at the police station next door to the church yard. He chastised himself for being such a coward. He was thinking they could get the police for him from the police station before he could get far. Of course, he had his pistol hidden in his jacket pocket. He wished he could have sneaked out his double barrel to but that had to stay home. Mary's hand clasped his face gently outside the car window "I'm going to pray for you that you can be healed. Pray that you can forget that village". Uncle Bob's hand felt for the security of the gun inside his pocket. She told Donna to go ahead and she stood there with the rosary in her hand until they drove off. Her uncle stared with faded, empty, eyes out the now rolled up window. He was being guarded by an impatient Sophia.

Donna had more than one route to get to the Psychiatric Hospital, at St. Ann's: the Betham Highway, or the Eastern Main Road? Donna knew that the smoke and stench choking the Betham highway was at its worse lately. Almost every week there was some fire at the landfill belching out toxic walls of smoke.

The Protest

At the Barataria roundabout she saw horrid polluted smoke spreading in the air over the Betham highway.

"Seeds of our destruction," she said sotto voce. She knew that at mourning time the eastern main road would be gridlocked in traffic. The fastest route was to take the Lady Young Road which runs through Morvant. Her uncle was sick and she didn't want him stuck in traffic. They saw something was disrupting the traffic on Lady Young Road. "How do I get through this damn obstacle course?" Donna asked her two moping passengers.

She gripped her steering wheel and cursed as she passed the gas station. She saw two scruffy men drop an old refrigerator shell on the road in the middle of her path that had made her swerve to escape.

"What the hell?" she yelled as a police officer chased after the men. She observed that a few cars had hurried through the obstacles at Morvant junction so she wondered if she could do the same. She made tight curves expertly maneuvering around other debris left on the road. The two more police officers she saw had their own problems to pay her any attention. Seems no police would not be left to direct the traffic. The common way for residents to get media attention was to block the road with debris and light fires. She lowered the volume on her car deck and rolled down her window just a crack. Angry cries of police brutality were heard together with sirens some distance away. A harsh metallic scraping from front wheel made her suspect a piece of debris was now attached to her tire thus releasing the air in it. She pulled into an area clear of people and parked her car off the roadway. She got out the car apprehensively. She had guessed correctly that the tire was punctured. The tire had a piece of galvanized iron and two small nails stuck to it. "Watch Uncle Bob for me! Sophia? We have to change the tire." She asked her daughter frowning through the driver's window.

"He keeps repeating 'In the malice Matelot would freeze?' Sophia replied as she carried down her window.

"I'll change the tire alone. Stay in the car." Donna said sternly knowing that Sophia would be eager to get out of the car and have a look at the protest. Donna hunched on the bonnet of the car astonished as she watched the police beat a protester.

"They're protesting because a thirteen-year-old boy was shot by the police. Police said the boy had fired at them. But there was no gun found on the boy, mom" Sophia told her mother as she got out of the car. She remembered what she had heard in school. One of the form two students in her school had been shot by police. He was in one of the top Morvant drug gangs. He was a witness to underhand dealing by some corrupt cops.

"Ok since you're out of the car you can help me lift out the spare from the trunk."

In between the protest a woman scuffled with and choked one of the police officers. Violence broke out as other protesters clashed with the few lightly armed police officers that arrived. Bottles and rocks hurtled dangerously through the air; intended on wounding the police officers. The loud cursing and violence destroyed whatever hope there was of peace in the tense situation. Frantic sirens penetrated the chaos. Some boys in their school uniform came up to Donna's stranded car. "Give we something and we go fix yuh car." said the most audacious one of them.

"It's ok we don't need help it's just a flat tire." Donna replied nonchalantly, as she looked at her uncle who remained in the backseat of the car.

They were staring lustfully at Donna's body and saying what they would do to her private parts. She felt a little intimidated now, she new she always dressed in a titillating manner.

"Is ah slap that you're lookin for?" Donna shot out angrily.

"Sophia! Get in de car" she yelled. She went around to the trunk to get her tools. Donna shrieked as a speeding Ambulance ripped her door mirror off. The car was pelted with gravel by the ambulance tires.

The boys ran off laughing at the Donna's loss. The ambulance pulled to the side of the road a little way ahead. The paramedics were waiting for police protection to pick up an unconscious victim; a police officer. Everyone took cover as gunmen on nearby hills began shooting. The few struggling police had to wait until other officers with machine guns arrived. Hopeful their backup could get through the hail of bullets. Uncle Bob scrambled to the driver's seat and started his niece's car.

Donna ripped open the back door and jumped in. Uncle Bob looked back at his niece through the rear-view mirror. He saw a scared and frustrated look on Donna's face. "Listen dear, I have not gone insane. I swear to you I'm not mad. We must get out of here. I can take us out of this protest. Uncle Bob floored the gas violently covering the sedan in a furious dust. He swerved dangerously onto the road he spun the car around to head out of the lady young back to Barataria. He expertly maneuvered his way on the shoulder of the road when he had to avoid approaching police jeeps. As gunfire from the hills became sporadic delinquent protesters threw firecrackers to confuse the police. Uncle Bob parked the car in an empty street in Barataria and got out of the car, away from the chaos. It was a long time since he had that much excitement." Is everyone ok?" Uncle Bob asked.

"Yes, we're alright."

"Help me Fix the tire quickly Sophia. That's it we're going back home." Donna decided.

"What about school Mom?" Sophia asked. Donna couldn't give an answer to Sophia.

Uncle Bob held his niece's shoulder firmly before she got in the car. He kept her out of the car seemingly lost for words.

"I have a little insight into what goes on with you and aunty. I feel sorry…" She confessed, breaking the silence. She placed a gentle arm on her Uncle's shoulder. She felt she had analyzed the situation with her uncle.

"You can tell me if I'm wrong, but this is what I suspect. Your wife and daughter keep you like a prisoner in that house. That's why you tried to start your old car and run away. I toot my horn on mornings when I pass by your house. You usually wave to me while wiping the dew off your daughter's car. That must be all they allow you to do around your house. Am I right? I heard Aunty doesn't even trust you to light the stove. I know it may seem like they are treating you like a child but maybe they are afraid you burn yourself or worst. I'm certain you won't intentionally harm yourself of course. We will talk more later I'm taking you to my house for coffee, away from this mess, ok." Uncle Bob trusted her reassuring voice.

"Sherlyn had a baby in Matelot we didn't know about until we went up there, the day after her drowning. He should be about twenty by now, old enough to know the heartless decisions we made back then. We decided not to tell anyone because the child was not her husband's. We just abandoned him, and then our unkindness reigned supreme over our compassion. I went through a lot of changes in my life since then. I also want to express to him the regret I feel, if I could find him." Uncle Bob lamented.

"Maybe I can withstand another day without losing the rest of my sanity, not to mention my teeth, but you have to hear my story. No one else would listen." Uncle Bob persisted with a weak smile.

"The spare is on mom you could continue discussing things later." Her daughter interrupted. Inside the car Uncle Bob started to tell of his troubles.

"It's been a long time, but it was her face I saw. I went into my old workshop to read my newspapers as I usually do. I saw an article about a place that for many years I had avoided. The place is piscatorial village called Matelot. The village healer was in the article. She said some creepy things that got to me. She said that the land was dying of exposure to a chill. It is ironic that she was mentioned as the village healer; the sight of her made me sick. Imagine that, her name after it was blocked out all these years in my mind. Here look at her picture." His trembling hand pulled out a crumpled Polaroid from his pocket. Donna took her eyes off the road to glance at the picture.

"Whose face is this?" Donna puzzled. Uncle Bob called a name but it was understated. She handed the clipping to a curious Sophia. Sophia thought the person had wise eyes. It was the first time she had heard Uncle Bob talk with enthusiasm.

"I was young, but I remembered when Sherlyn married that bus driver from the country, at San Juan

RC." Donna said realizing it was about Sherlyn that her uncle Bob was troubled. "My daughter died in Matelot, Donna. I thought I could forget her death and move on but lately it's all I can think about. I even had been visited by some very dark nightmares. That healer of Matelot is the only one who can give my mind peace, before my life is over. She was my daughter's mother-in-law. She once wanted to say something about why my daughter's life had ended so tragically; but we would not let the perfect image of our daughter be spoiled. Our pain, because of some cruel destiny, turned to hate for Ma Ethelrida. Our pride caused dissension between families, so up to now we remain ignorant of the truth. I think I'm ready to hear what Ma Ethelrida has to say. Now that time has passed, I don't want to blame the poor lady for the death of my girl. She just had some things to say about Sherlyn that we couldn't deal with at that time. Let me go to her home and talk to her Judy, please. I am begging. She has a story to tell about Sherlyn. I want to hear this macabre tale before I meet my end. I'm going up there and beg her to forgive us for our antipathy towards her. Your Aunty blamed Ma Ethelrida for our daughter's death. She said Ma Ethelrida was a witch who had sacrificed her daughter. My wife became a member of a Christian group up there. The same group that was in the Matelot church on the day Sherlyn died. A villager told them that Ma Ethelrida practiced witchcraft on our daughter. Senior Members of the group told my wife what they heard after Sherlyn's death. This group talks to her almost daily on the phone.

I fear they are really a dark order, a cult of some sort; and not really the Christians that they claim. That is why I don't dare tell my wife I want to go back up there. She believes a curse would befall me there. Matelot was the place where Mary, Sherlyn and I went; since I had to repair a P.A. system for the church. I don't know if the village wanted us or we marched voluntarily to our demise. Sherlyn found her future husband there. That same day my wife got introduced to some people, but they were not who they seemed. Her association with them would change us for the worst. Sherlyn would meet big Jim in Port of Spain as often as she could, and my wife would spend too much time with that cult group. I don't believe in blessings or curses. I want to accept the facts in my own way. The facts about how my child passed so unhappily from this world. You could say I became by degrees over the years the skeptic for whom my wife sees a future in hell for. Sherlyn's body having never been found leaves many questions to torment those who love her. Everyone helped us search even the parish priest up there who last saw her. She also had a son we abandoned. I hope he will talk to me in spite of the wrong we did."

"I want to help but Aunty thinks that sometimes you cannot differentiate between fantasy and reality." Donna said, and her mind grappled with what her uncle said.

"Donna this is what happened. I made up my mind to go Matelot in search of answers. We have foolishly cheated our selves of answers. You won't understand how every day I hear the same questions about Sherlyn in my head. But my wife shouldn't make representations of delusion. She is so a cult member that she threw away a glass I got as a gift simply because it had the zodiac symbol, of Capricorn, on it. She would not drink or eat from Orisha or Hindu people as if their food could poison her somehow. She repeats Light and Ice on the phone sometimes for two minutes. She is just so crazy. In the night she imagines that there are evil beings outside the house and starts praying for the light and ice to protect her. Do you know how irritating that is, to have someone mumbling prayers in your ears when you're trying to sleep. This assignation must happen, I need some answers to keep my sanity! Will you help me meet Ma Ethelrida one last time?" Uncle Bob fought to keep his voice steady and calm. Donna sensed that he had loved his daughter and could not forget.

"Despite twenty years having past since her daughter's death, her mind is mired in superstitious mumble jumble. I am sane as you. Look Donna I am getting my answers one way or the other!" Bob hoped he was poignant enough to convince Donna.

"I'll try to help. Your dad will kill me Sophia. Uncle Bob we're going up to Matelot. How long would the drive be?"

"Two and a half hours, Donna." Uncle Bob smiled eagerly.

"Mom, this is crazy, and dad will kill us." Sophia said astonished that her mother agreed to go Matelot.

"Afraid you would miss your little girlfriends at school? Shut up!" Donna sneered at Sophia.

"This darling niece of mine is all I have." Donna blushed at what uncle Bob said.

"Let's assume this trip is going to take place. I'm in school uniform mom. You do remember this is a school day right mom?"

"It's an emergency dare", Donna answered, and Uncle Bob zoned off in his own thoughts.

The Trapped

When Sherlyn came to Matelot everyone wanted to know who she was, and when she started to live there. They thought she was a very beautiful woman. It is ironic that now the villagers who left must be in a town like San Juan, while she stays trapped there in Matelot. Sherlyn lamented *in here I don't need to eat. I think I am not aging either. I can read time from this entity's precise clock. My life is just suspended in a lingering, tenacious sleep. Deep within my heart I still yearn for the strength to wake. I want to awake from this. This iceberg is an impervious prison that I can't escape, no matter my will. I remember during last year's hurricane I prayed for strong waves to smash this ice with trashing Caribbean water. Since the accident I've been trapped here twenty years now. I think time is running out because the world outside is becoming like the iceberg.*

Sometimes she dreamt of being on the outside walking on the beach. In her ice prison she saw the small waves lapping this holographic place. She saw turtles, dolphins, some stingray, and brown sea-weed passing around her. The water had changed dramatically though within recent times. It turned to an icy poison. She saw fish float about lifeless with the cursed blobs of ice. She didn't even hear the drone of boat engines anymore or see *iridescent* boat fuel on the water. It was a foreboding of the end, to have only this holographic winter season, and feeling of dread. She doubted that her mother in-law has left knowing the resilient person that Ma Ethelrida was. Ma Ethelrida would rather live in this freezing village, with the house and coast that she loved, than anywhere else. She has never even been to Tobago- the closest island to Trinidad, its sister isle. Ma Ethelrida came to San Juan for the wedding and took the first car back to Matelot which became available; not even spending the night at Sherlyn's house. Ma Ethelrida said she had to go turn on her house lights and feed her animals, so she couldn't stay. Sherlyn tried to talk to her sometimes from the ice; at times when her mother in law might be quietly lying in bed, or when her incense had calmed the whole house. However, Sherlyn didn't know for sure if Ma Ethelrida heard her telepathic cries. Sherlyn knew Ma Ethelrida had not forgotten her, and Sherlyn did not doubt Ma Ethelrida had truly forgiven her.

She eventually realized there were two other people captured, in compartments, here with her. There was a man and a woman from an older time in history. They were trapped here maybe five hundred years before Sherlyn. The man's name was Lord Merwittek and the woman was Kathi. They were mortal enemies of each other. Before he was trapped here the man came with ships, soldiers, and priests to her world. He spoke many languages. He wanted a mythical tree of immortality and every piece of gold from the islands. He and everyone he brought did evil things to the aboriginal people they found. He was welcomed by the indigenous people kindness and admiration. The people who lived on the island tried to please him with everything they had. But he was a greedy psychopath, without any empathy. He made them find gold or they would risk losing arms and limbs. He and his men raped their women and killed their babies. The priest he brought terrified them with his sadistic preaching. His power was greater than Sherlyn's. He was in this ice longer than her, so he had more time to learn how to channel its power. He used the ice to broadcast messages telepathically. He broadcasts to a small group of prominent men across the globe. He repeats a lie to them. She would hear him repeat this lie frequently. It was mind programming with awe and hidden meaning for his disciples. He looped the crazy tale over and over until it becomes truth in his subjects' brain. The mental broadcast is a type of pseudo-Christian history. It starts off *in heaven, in the kingdom of God. In heaven the iceberg was there, as Lucifer, singing in the choir. Lucifer generated dances of frequencies for praising God. He was startled when he heard other angels sing, in praise of God, for the first time. His music made the angels more conscious. The voices were not truly harmonious he discerned. He could separate distinctly each voice in the choir. Then some angels talked to him while others continued to sing. They asked him why he was so beautiful, and why he was so intelligent, and if they should praise him also. To answer them he tried what no other creation could do; communicate directly with his god, the hidden entity. He took pity on the other angels and asked the hidden presence why he was made more beautiful than the vast number of angels. He wanted to get the answers for the angels that pestered him. His probing of things was always arrested. He felt his wisdom had stopped growing. He counseled all the angels who would listen to abhor their present state. They prepared themselves to leave heaven easily hypnotized by the intense conviction of the Lucifer. Soon a revolt in heaven began. The rebel Lucifer roared in savage anger at God, the hidden. Angels fought against angels in a war in heaven. Heaven slipped from under Lucifer's charging feet making him disorientated. He was confused as all light but his was extinguished. He was dreaming it all. Heaven was all his own creation. Infernal with rage Lucifer stretched in every direction to chase away the darkness and reached its limit with the darkness still unfathomed. He could only know his own mind nothing else.*

It questioned 'what was it that I wanted? why am I gazing out to the void? It was there before I heard music. Has the darkness made me into a fading light to be extinguished forever? What made me yesterday, and then left this dreamy mind? Did this darkness conceive me at its pleasure?' it spat out to the emptiness. It pained it hungered to know his beginning. It abused its imagination separate itself more from the darkness that choked it. It had to create a new universe where it could rule. Its emotions cooled and dust was made. It made various intelligent life forms to come out of the dust to provide it with answers to the meaningless emptiness.' The grand architect sent shockwaves to clouds of dust to collapse them. It made Earth capture the elements of life, like carbon baked in red stars. When it formed the Earth, it dived into it as a comet. The comet never disintegrated but took the semblance of an iceberg.

Earth generates millions of types of plants, animals, and microorganisms but now man dominates because we were made the cleverest. It wants man to gain more territory in the universe, but it warns that the sun will not keep itself balanced against gravity forever; to give humankind the time needed to colonize the solar system and many light years beyond. It asks 'Do we have the tolerance to co-operate? And will we reach the level of scientific wizardry needed to shatter the limits of speed?' it warns because our advance to the heavens has been too slow man stands no chance of surviving the mass extinction countdown; as ninety nine percent of all species that have lived on the Earth faced; fit and sick, old and young. It commands that the weak must be massacred to make room for a newer genetic programming, languages and technologies. The time Lucifer gave to Humanity to understand the universe is almost up. Man has seen his fragile planet rise above the bleak grayness of the lunar landscape, but terrorism, corruption, and poverty burdens Homo sapiens. As man lay the world to waste this creator is manifesting himself deeper into reality. It will start the cataclysmic process, to destroy humans; beginning as an iceberg in a little forgotten village. This iceberg did not fall from the foot of a mountain but was made to annihilate worlds. It is a type of sensor. Its body is in the Earth sensing and reacting to man's pollution. The dust carries acids, radioactive materials from atomic bomb testing, and toxic chemicals from irresponsible monopolies. The worldwide deforestation, sterilizing of lands, cancers, and diversion of water by man must be halted. If time runs out for man, we will leave behind deep sea creatures as the dominators of Earth. But our part of the dream is almost over the iceberg waits to trigger humankind's annihilation. While we dream at most for an hour or two, it spends the life span of worlds dreaming. It was dreaming before the universe, before heaven, and whatever reaches the limit of human description and dimensions. Its whole existence is dreaming. This physical universe is another dream of it. If man is a successful creation maybe, then it doesn't have to dream anymore.

They would hear an iceberg groaning, then he would continue the rest of the gibberish to his group. "Soon this iceberg will release me when the time is right. I will take charge to stop this destruction of Earth. You can call me Lord Merwittek. I will build an army of machines to serve our purposes. My machines will depopulate the Earth, so only the best of mankind will survive. The iceberg will favor my machines and slow its hand of destruction on the Earth. I am the only one who can communicate with the iceberg; with Lucifer. Only under me, you the chosen few will gain the whole Earth, and its resources. If I die all is lost for mankind. In time our machines will travel through the solar system to gain more worlds for us. We are the only one's worthy of living on Earth the rest of humanity is to be wiped out, like I wiped out many primitives when I once walked the Earth."

Sherlyn thought he is trying to convince, his followers on the outside, that Lucifer is god; who created our planets life with a comet strike to the Earth. But she knew God was within her, and God was not some rock from space, and Lucifer is not god. The lie was coming from a dark lord. To build his empire he must gain all the territory of Earth. The truth is we are not durable to survive the radiation of space for hundreds even thousands of years. We can only see the visible spectrum of light, and we are blind to the deadly types of radiation. To pass the barrier around the Earth would almost be impossible. So, he wants to control machines remotely from computers on Earth. Only our machines can survive space since radiation will reach inside our skulls. Humans physically must stay well below 1000 miles barrier. Our DNA cannot randomly learn to stop radiation. His goal is to use science to turn humans into part machines in the hopes of colonizing space. He hides the fact that an inner advance to consciousness will take us out to the stars.

Sherlyn found out the iceberg was really a freezing weapon. It was used by advance life forms to freeze stars. The extinguished stars would then become ringed planets like Saturn. But worlds had collided in cosmological chaos and the alien weapon was ejected out of its target, dwarf star. It became attracted to our planet because Earth had potential for a certain kind of life, and it sped towards us. It had wreaked havoc through our solar system destroying a planet before it landed quietly on Earth. By the time the aliens got back to see the results of their weapon; they had lost it, as it was on our planet Earth, and not in the little sun they had chosen.

During the great flood on Earth it captured some people. They were released from the ice eventually, but have died out over time. The other person there trapped in the iceberg was Kathi - from Lord Merwittek's time, she was born in South America. She came to Trinidad for a few days to look for special plants. There was a plague spreading that made pus, coughing and high fever then sure death. A lot of her people were dying. She was sent to find medicine to help the different tribal areas and cities- from Santa Cruz to Chihuahua. She had gathered up her collection plants, the she found a group of infected Amerindian men, by the mouth of the river. They were very sick with high fever. She gave them some of her medicines. She thought they might be able to recover. One of them in her care propped himself up against a tree and started pointed out to the sea. He said he was seeing a blue cave floating in the water nearby. She thought he was hallucinating but he was seeing the iceberg entity. When she was leaving them close to the Matelot River, she spotted Lord Merwittek's caravel. It was too late to hide since the dangerous men on the ship had already spotted her canoe. They came near and tried to call her on the ship, hoping to capture her. When Lord Merwittek's evil eyes locked on hers, she cursed him. She would never give him the knowledge he sought from her. She aimed and fired her arrow at him. He tried to duck but was too slow. His men fired immediately on her canoe. She hit him in the chest. Their shot smashed the front of her canoe and tossed her in the water. She thought how all her plants were lost and now a lot of her people will die of the sickness. She felt hopelessness now. She was treading in the water when to her pleasant surprise Lord Merwittek's men throw him overboard, still living but shot with an arrow. His men were glad to abandon him to drown- they thought that he did not pay them enough gold and he was mad for chasing a fabled tree of immortality. She swam to him and fought with him to drown him. Then they both were captured by the iceberg.

Kathi was also more powerful than Sherlyn because she had more mental abilities; was more creative, balanced and knowledgeable. Little by little Sherlyn's ability emerged to send telepathic bulletins to her loved ones. She called to them to find her. She believed that that her father would still come for her even after twenty years of captivity. The iceberg was a time bomb that already had its triggering input. She knew the only person that could disturb the iceberg to threshold was her Jokull. He had to have been far away from Matelot, because of all the years she searched for his mind and only found emptiness. She would keep trying and if he was back, she would communicate with him.

She hoped to be free soon before it was too late for mankind. She didn't see herself as the savior of humankind, but she deciphered a little of what the entity had written on it, she thought that would be enough to help her stop the coming cataclysm.

The Village

They stopped by a fast food outlet in Valencia to buy lunch although Uncle Bob didn't like the delay. He also did not eat fast foods because of additives like monosodium glutamate. He did not drink sodas either because he was sure that corporations did not care if they poisoned him with sugar. Twenty years ago, when uncle bob and Mary were here to join the search for their daughter, there had been a crowd waiting to see them. The curious villagers had been very friendly and helpful. They volunteered their pirogues and villagers even dived in the water. They searched the last beach where she was seen; they searched the river mouth, and they followed the sea currents, but they found nothing. There had been no helicopter search for his daughter, but the coast guard had used one of their boats, for a day. The sad search had led to nothing. His heart had sunk to his stomach. There was so much disappointment back then, Uncle Bob thought. He was so close now he could almost here his daughter.

Back then he left in a prayerful mood leaving it up to God, instead of pursuing it with all our forces. Now if he didn't find her Uncle Bob would leave here inconsolable, ready to die. He thought what she would be now if she was found in the ice. He empathized with Ma Ethelrida who had all the blame dumped on her. He wondered how much of his life he will be able to rebuild, because he was an old man already. Donna listened to her favorite Bollywood music as she drove. She thought about her ex boyfriend and decided to meet him soon. She wondered if to call her husband's number. She thought it might cause another argument and decided against it. She wanted something different from the same old boring day she would spend at work or home with Ted. Sophia decided that this was a good break from school as she listened to her melancholic gothic pieces, through shorting headphones, stored on her mobile phone. On the way there were damaged roads from Valencia to Toco. The damaged roads dogged their progress and reminded Donna how dead her front shocks were. Uncle Bob noticed from Grande Riviere onward that the dense, luxuriant, equatorial rain forest was progressively being invaded by alien cold temperate coniferous trees. Tropical plant communities were diseased and sparse among thriving populations of spruce, birch, rowan, and aspen as they closed on Matelot.

"Most of the local trees are sick and dying. This forest looks strange because there should be closely packed trees with creepers and vines strangling them.

Instead there are rows of pines." Uncle Bob remarked with awe.

"Are you sure our local trees weren't replanted with pines?" Donna had enough time to observe the trees because she had to drive slowly. Before the village the coastal road narrowed with sixteen separate land slippages. Donna frowned wary of the crumbling Matelot road, and its one-foot deep water gorged sides. Uncle Bob said the road and the village would soon disappear into the sea. The sea water was the destabilizing influence on the soil. Desperately needed repairs were not being done by the local government or the ministry of works and transport. Maybe it would be better if private individuals pooled some money and labor and fix it themselves.

At Shark River they encountered members of the army. The soldiers were crossing a few people over the wide river out of Matelot. The haggard looking people were heading south; anyway, away from the village they lived in all their lives. Their heavy bags, furniture and appliance pieces tested the robustness of the temporary bridge erected. Recently a truck trying to cross the river had crashed through the original bridge, destroying it. The driver had swum out lucky and unhurt. He lamented on the riverbank that this place was blighted by unbelievers. His truck was carrying equipment for the church; including heavy copper cables and electrical equipment. His bible fell into the water unnoticed by him. Donna left her car on the southern side of the river. She was lightheaded from the long drive and a diesel scent along the riverbank, from the crashed truck. They blundered across the temporary bridge of makeshift wooden planks. The soldiers were talking among themselves about a riot that broke out in Morvant. Trudging up and down the slippery riverbank left there army boots heavy with mud.

The mist that floated on the bank felt like cold, unsettling fingers on uncle bob's spine. The coldness was felt through every stitch of their clothing. A crepuscular level of light reached the ground through the arching bamboo plants. They watched the road go from pavement to gravel to mud to a footpath through enclosing jungle.

A little way from the river they saw David a thirty something year old man tooting his horn enthusiastically at them. He had been waiting to be hired.

"Hello, Good afternoon; where do you folks want to go?" he offered animatedly trying to contrast with the sad looking people they were seeing, leaving across the bridge. Uncle Bob had surveyed David - the man before him dressed in heavy wool clothing, registered as out of place here. David was too young and bright to stay in that soul killing place, the village had become.

"We want to reach a little after the Catholic Church. Are you going there?" Uncle Bob asked apprehensively.

"Of course, I'll take you there. My name is David but people here, what's left of them call me Bounty." he responded kindly. Inside the van Uncle Bob saw his driver's license permit which said David Kelly. Uncle Bob's pistol became exposed for a brief moment long enough for Donna to see it, and her mouth to drop open in surprise. Sophia covered her mouth with her hands. Donna then locked eyes with Sophia and silently told her to shush with her head movement, as Sophia noticed the gun to.

"Only very few people have chosen to stay in this village. Today I dropped off a few more people by the bridge, they were leaving for good. Life is harder than before and getting worse. You have to survive on your own crops but the weather is so unkind. Of course I know a lady who is a fighter and vows she'll never leave. Me and her are the only protectors of this village. There's a nefarious group here that we battle. They have stolen the church, and they have long driven out the sincere Christians. They dabble in the dark arts, and they could destroy this village." David told them.

"I disagree this place hints at a gothic landscape just like my album covers. The weird is beautiful to me sometimes. All that is missing here now is some dark castle. I am Sophia by the way." Sophia naively rebutted. "There is no castle Dracula in this case young lady, but the leader of the cult here is equal to Dracula, I think. Did you know your name means wisdom?" David said. Uncle Bob had his own suspicions about the people at that church.

"So, nothing has changed then. That wretched cult has ruined our lives although we live far from them. They have control over my wife. After I meet with my friend living here, I want to go see that church." Uncle Bob interrupted Sophia from answering David.

"Are you guys staying here overnight?" David asked.

"Yes. We will be staying over at my friends" Uncle Bob answered.

"Who is your friend by the way? If you don't mind me asking. I know everyone here on a first name basis. Not much people now though; I can check all the original residents on one hand." David was very curious to know who they knew there in Matelot.

"Do you know the aged fair skinned lady who sells herbal medicines here? Her son used to drive the government bus." Uncle Bob studied David's face as he asked.

"Yes, I do. We are not far from her. Ma Ethelrida like ah mother to me. Many times, in need I slept under her roof. many times! Her real son disappeared twenty years ago." David responded earnestly.

"Then we've met the right man!" Donna exclaimed.

"I am glad for, my friend Ma Ethelrida, you seem like an honest young man" Uncle Bob told David. David told them the story of the wolves for their own safety. He remembered the dangerous pack of wolves; he thought were stray dogs that attacked him by the beach yesterday evening. The wolves came out from nowhere and tried to surround him. The harsh pounding of the surf augmented the growls they made. He was really worried because they were too big and wild looking to be dogs. He had to make a mad dash for his van. The biggest wolf pounced on the door of the van seconds after he slammed it shut. The air had smelt pungent. The wolves took turns snarling and spitting on the van's rolled up glass. David still saw the snapping jaws. In the tray of the van he had fish from Toco wrapped in newspaper. They had snatched it up hungrily. He hadn't seen any of the normal type of strays for weeks. The wolves that tried to catch him were huge; at least five feet in length. He hadn't heard a bird sing in weeks. Most of the time the only people who came here were hikers or tourist who had wandered to far from Toco bay. He wondered who else saw these big predators. David's passengers had noticed streets empty of cars and people. The silence fitted the dull colors and bleak, oppressive atmosphere.

Donna hoped not to encounter those big stray animals. On the way uncle Bob showed Sophia how Samuel and Pyke Street was leaning almost enough to tumble and take the church and closed school below, down into the sea. The crotons in the yards they passed were all glossy and blackened as if it was being killed by a frost.

Ma Ethelrida's House

"Whey de white monster boi? We hah to find tha thing!" Brent said to Danny. They would spend the night at the church to pick up the drugs coming by boat.

"Yeah boi! Leh we check by tanty! Ah feel he go smell she food." Danny suggested.

"Awright we go go! Ah know we hit him, yuh know, baw he run before ah geh more shots off." Brent agreed to search by Ma Ethelrida's house.

Ma Ethelrida surveyed the sky. She saw that the normally overcast sky was a little bright today; it was even warm- like the days before this curse started. She could still see the dead ginger lily plants fencing a side of the yard. The weeds were scanty as if plants couldn't benefit from sunlight and the rainfall here. The place was strangely devoid of common plants that flourished in other parts of the island. Maybe if there were more fine days like this, things would grow a little. She sat down in her cedar chair and fell into a shallow sleep.

A white shaggy man-bear creature was watching Ma Ethelrida beyond the fence. It had already dined on three big rats minutes ago. Its jaws hung open and foamy saliva and rat's blood kept spilling out, splotching its chin. Its blue eyes were mad with rage. The hole in its right shoulder was bleeding and burning. With closed eyes Ma Ethelrida slapped at the insect that was biting her and woke herself. The temperature had dropped quickly since she fell asleep, and she woke up shivering. The little animals she kept in cages began to go berserk with terror. The snow beast broke into a run towards her. Ma Ethelrida stood petrified at the sight of the advancing Yeti-like beast. Brent's van ran over one of the many wolves sniffing on the road; following the rampaging man-bear creature. The wolf made a squeal and sickening thumping sound below the floor of the van. Danny looked back and through the back glass he saw the mangled animal.

"Oh gawd we hit ah wolf!" Danny shouted gleefully. A footpath of gravel led to Ma Ethelrida's little rusted gate, at the foot of a narrow porch step. Brent drove furiously through Ma Ethelrida's yard. Ma Ethelrida was on the floor of her porch screaming, about to be mauled by the thick furred snowman. The van stopped inches before the steps. Danny grabbed a short length of mora wood, from below the step, to hit the beast with. With agility he scaled up the porch banister skipping over the steps. He swung the weapon in a good arc. The snow beast was struck soundly on the head. It rocked, shook off the blow, and spun around at him. It flashed hateful eyes and teeth. Its body was bulging with strong, confident muscles. It leaped at him, a bullet from Brent's gun shattered its skull in mid flight and it fell through the front door, in a bloody mess. The French door's glass panes were broken, and a dead creature's paws were sticking through. The curious wolves scrambled into some bushes. The pact of wolves made strange noises.

"Oh gomm de big white monster bite meh arm." Ma Ethelrida managed to say panting for breath and holding her arm in pain.

"oou guude! Oou guude! Yuh ent see tha! It spin rong tuh bite!" Danny said breathlessly to Brent.

"yeah boi baw you eh see ah hit it?" Brent responded.

"Tanty this is ah monster! We takin it dong by d church! And yuh kno dey doh like you?"

"Thank yuh fuh saving me." Ma Ethelrida said. Brent and Danny strained with the shaggy snow beast and hoisted it unto their van tray.

"I carryin dis by Delling and ask'em 'boss wha we could geh fuh dis?'" Brent told Danny as they were driving away. David passed the two narcos as he pulled into Ma Ethelrida's yard. He saw something like a white ape in the tray of their van.

Donna got out and ran out to help Ma Ethelrida.

"Are you ok Aunty?" she asked as she soothed Ma Ethelrida with her hands, as a shocked Sophia looked on.

"Oh gawm David! they had a snow monster here. Brent shoot it. Yuh will see about it eh? Look and make sure nuttin doh come back! yuh hear?" Ma Ethelrida said as she limped into the dark drawing room, with Donna helping her. Sophia turned on the lights. David peered anxiously through each window.

"Once you ok Ma then I will go and scout around." David said. Donna found the first aid kit and bandaged up her arm. Luckily it was not a deep bite. Ma Ethelrida was still trembled with fear; remembering the glee in the beast's ravenous eyes. She dusted off her hands and blouse neurotically. On a dark oak wooden cabinet, through the gauzy like yellowish lightning, Uncle Bob made out a picture of his beloved daughter. He was surprised the house did not seem dark and oppressive even though his daughter must have had some painful times here. From the roof to the floorboard Uncle Bob could see the house's losing battle with land slippages, in the form of long fissures along the garish, mint colored walls of the house. The house was built by Ma Ethelrida's late husband. He had gotten the piers for the house from a stack of abandoned wooden telephone poles. The floorboards were from a renovated house in Curepe. The galvanize iron for the roof came from a renovated shop by the R.C. church. It was a humble two-bedroom house made it to accommodate simple and ordinary folks.

"Here! Take my gun David! I can't run after those wolves and monsters like you can." Uncle Bob suggested and handed David his gun. David did not plan on going far, there were too many dangers there presently. He would just move the dead wolf from the middle of the road and see if anymore wolves or snow beasts were near the premises. Before he left David warned them about the coldness there.

"This morning I found big chunks of crystal-clear ice on the shore. Remember if you have to spend the night here this place gets breath-catching icy at times. I hope you have warm clothes. I examine my hands, feet, ears, nose whenever I awake from sleep. Do you know what I look for? I look for frost bite. People have lost a heel, half a foot, or piece of ear up here, due to a mysterious frigid touch. Some have blamed it on a strange mist they have seen creeping around our houses. There are stories that an iceberg that you can find a little out to sea is the culprit, for all the ills this village has seen recently. Branches of trees are breaking off because of ice collecting on it. Make sure and cloak up good before going out at night. I'll be back soon!" He was so glad, to see lively people from outside the village, hence he had to open up.

"Sure David, be careful out there!" Uncle Bob called out to David. The well swept floorboards creaked under David's feet as he left hastily to dispose of the carcass, and to scare away the other strays. Donna and Uncle Bob shut all the doors and windows after he drove away.

Origins

Ma Ethelrida hugged Uncle Bob. "How long has it been? This place cold now but at least you finally away, Bobby. You made it!" her voice had recovered some of its strong and hypnotic character.

"I haven't been here since we searched… twenty years ago. Thank you for responding to my letters. Thank you for helping me." Uncle Bob's words were not steady.

"I am sorry about your wife" Ma Ethelrida lamented.

"I need forgiveness from you. I am ready now to atone. The years have passed but I have not really been living. It is like I have been under a spell. I am glad to be away from Mary I think she has a lot to do with my zombie like existence. But do not worry lady; say what you want to say. You have done nothing wrong. We have wronged you." Bob lamented in earnest.

"I will forgive you seventy times seventy. Bearing a grudge only destroys what chance there is of making sense of this thing."

"Mary try to put me in d madhouse jus today! She rel good yes. She is a rel trap. I'm past being polite to that terminator. I believe you about the influence of that cult she is in, that light and ice shit is so sickening!" Uncle Bob answered.

"We can't run anymore; the future is pulling us to it. It has to be a good future because we are all here together. The world is at stake, but I can't be pessimistic with you here. Now you can hear my side of the story, face to face. I could have gone so far away from the bad memories this place was charged with. It took all my will to stay here alone. And now you meet a woman fatigued by the unnatural coldness of the village. I am always coughing and feverish. I could have moved to Sangre Grande and open up a shop; when my surroundings took on its dreadful change. I am a fighter, and I will battle hard for my home. I need you Bobby for this fight; we face the greatest foe ever." Ma Ethtlerida confessed melancholically.

"Sherlyn talks to me in my dreams about the iceberg. I have back up for this battle. This warrior princess is Donna my niece, and the young lady is Sophia her daughter." Donna and Sophia smiled sincerely.

"Thank you for bandaging me. Donna you must be a very special person to help him come up here. He tried to come for almost two years but could not get away." Ma Ethelrida said admiringly with a warm smile as her eyes focused on Uncle Bob.

"Aunty you are welcome it was no trouble at all. Aunty, I'm just glad for Uncle Bob, he can get his closer on Sherlyn and find out about his grand son. I just didn't know the situation he was in. I would have sneaked him here sooner. Today had so many revelations. And you and David are the proud protectors of this place. Anyhow I would listen to Uncle Bob from now on; he seems to really believe in what he is saying." Donna said earnestly.

"Uncle Bob worked his charms on my mom to get away from Aunty Mary." Sophia said.

"I'm glad you found David he is a nice person; like a son to me. I had no real comfort here for years after Big Jim varnished, but when David and I make friends, David would do everything to help me. David would keep me company and help me with my work. I thought him everything I knew; about the changes that would come here. You guys and David save meh life. Thank you!" Ma Ethelrida said.

"It was hard for us not to find David he was the sole taxi here. This village is emptied out." Uncle Bob said.

"This village has shrunken a lot. The village population is the smallest I have ever seen. Here lies disaster. I have seen houses, thousands of dollars worth of fish, and crops left to rot away by their owners. I can count on one hand the families that remain here. A few years ago, we were catching healthy shark, carite, and cro cro to supply the nation. You had good fish catch for the Lenten period. Now the fish here gets you sick. The fish here contains poisons; I've experienced it firsthand." Ma Ethelrida remembered how a meal of fried fish- caught in Matelot a few days ago, made her hallucinate. After eating the meal in front on her porch chair, she saw sharp glassy icicles hanging directly overhead on her ceiling. Then water from them began dripping pooled around a surge protector, for her fan, she had on the ground threatening to electrocute her, but he was paralyzed. She fell off the chair and passed out.

"I only eat fish from other places now. People who left have been begging their authorities to look into it but all they got were promises. I think the sun is varnishing here. I expect to wake up any day with the sun gone forever. The sweet, north eastern winds from the Atlantic and the bright heat of the Caribbean sun rays falter here but it just doesn't feel right to let this evil win." Ma ethelrida said.

Ma Ethelrida insisted on cooking lunch for them first before talking about Sherlyn. Donna followed her into the cramped kitchen, which was partitioned from the drawing room, to give a hand. The kitchen window had a beautiful view of the bay. But you always had the feeling that you might fall out the window because it was low.

"I am glad you're here to cheer away some of this cold" she called out to Sophia as she made lunch.

To Sophia's delight there was the smell of fish cooking; especially nice slices of king fish. A humble soup was also being made, with ingredients from Toco; of green bananas and pacro, to be served with coconut bake. Sophia still doubted what I was saying about the fish in this pristine bay. She couldn't believe that fishes would just wash up to shore; dead and rotting or containing hallucinogens. It was my job to get foodstuff from Toco for Ma Ethelrida. When the food was served, Ma Ethelrida had a chance to take the weight off her feet and she sat down, with a bottle of rum.

"To warm your blood and keep out the influence of the ice." She said as she offered rum to her guests. Ma Ethelrida twisted off the cap of the bottle breaking the seal. She tilted the bottle and offered some sprinkles of the rum to the well swept floorboards. The scent of rum filled the air as they ate; a smoky, molasses aroma that made them grope their minds for memories of festive occasions of the past. 'Ma Ethelrida said soup was the only thing she would eat with a spoon, because she was accustomed to eating with her bare fingers, since childhood. She said the food always tasted better with her fingers, than a spoon or fork.'

Ma Ethelrida toasted to prosperity and happiness for everyone. Ma Ethelrida implanted arctic imagery in their minds as they ate. Her words were laden with an impossibility- Matelot was freezing. The sound of Bach's '13th Invention' floated up from Donna's pocket, under the table. Donna eyed Uncle Bob and frantically groped for her mobile phone. Both knew who it was calling Donna's cell phone. Impatiently Uncle Bob demanded Donna's mobile phone knocking down and a nearby cocoyea broom as he reached for it.

"Hello?" Uncle Bob croaked.

"Where are you? I have been trying to call Donna for an hour. Did the doctor see you? Do you know a state of emergency has been called? People are rioting in Morvant."

"I saw an article with Ma Ethelrida in the newspaper two years ago. And now I'm here in Matelot, no thanks to you and your cult leader."

"You fool you would bring a curse on us going by that witch!" her voice was like a whip cracking. Uncle Bob handed the phone to Donna and signaled for her to take it off.

"Aunty I'm sorry, we're all ok." Donna said and hung up.

"She doesn't understand my spirituality so therefore I am an evil witch!" Ma Ethelrida had heard distinctly when Mary hissed out the word witch.

"Mary joined that cult group after Sherlyn disappeared. They took over our lives. And they turned us against you Ethelrida. I am sorry I was too confused at the time to discern anything."

"My son was loyal to your daughter. But he had his problems. He was not perfect. Your wife told me once 'Sherlyn was tricked by the son of a sucouya into coming to live in this God forsaken village'. She didn't give me a chance to defend my son and myself."

"Don't worry this time I don't agree with my wife. Sherlyn was always a free-spirited person like me! She loved our town. We pushed her out of her own home. We forced that marriage. We should have stayed out of her business."

"Ma Ethelrida tell us what happened to Sherlyn, at that young age. What made her marriage fall to pieces?"

Donna poured a drink of rum for herself and offered the bottle to Uncle Bob.

"I'll be glad to tell you. I am tired from waiting all these years. My son, Big Jim loved the rural lifestyle so he brought your daughter up here to live. Life in this village is a slow, quiet, and simple; in contrast with your 'bustling' towns of San Juan and Port of Spain. She quickly became bored of this village; especially as big Jim was on the road most of the time, driving the government's bus. I don't know if this made her depressed also. A troubled man named Jokull eventually entered Sherlyn's life through me. He was from Norway. He came with two others from his homeland; Brother Aquilo and Ivar. They all belonged to a cult although I didn't know it at the time. He did carvings with wood he would find in the bush or on the beach. He was graceful, tall and had long blond Rasta hair. The cult brought him from his native land to escape the winters. He had a deep fear of ice over there. Imagine that he would have died of fright if he had to spend another winter there. He said he feared specifically the ice of Norway; it started when he was a young child. I think the cult group that brought him here had experimented on him, as a baby, and programmed the fear of ice into his subconscious."

"Just like they programmed Mary!" Uncle Bob blurted out.

Ma Ethelrida nodded and continued "He was a little odd but not violent at all. He lived mostly by himself in a seaside shack. He did not work much with other people. He did work for me sometimes cleaning my yard, building cupboard or repairing the roof. He asked me to cook for him sometimes. He would give me some of his carvings in return, sometimes fish or provisions. His work is very artistic as you can see. All of the carvings I have here are his. Sherlyn would give him the food for me sometimes, which is how they met. I heard rumors from neighbors that on her long walks on the beach she would end up in Jokull's little boat. I couldn't believe what I was hearing at first. I was a coward because I couldn't find the courage to mention it to Big Jim. He has a destructive temper. It seems she was having an affair with Jokull when she got away from this house. I could have told her that it was wrong. I was part of my son's undoing because I didn't tell him. People in the village were too scared to tell him either. It broke my heart how their lives had turned out."

"But marriage is also an unnatural creation. People change and if love is gone maybe they should move on from each other. In marriage we pretend we are not two different people, that we have the same morality, and that the same things make us happy. The truth is each man; woman owns themselves and so owns their own bodies and thoughts. And it is true that the unconscious decides things long before the higher brain can process it. So, people follow their urges first and then think about who was hurt afterwards. That is if the erotic encounter would not deliberately be forgotten soon afterwards." Donna said.

"I know Big Jim never entertained the idea of living with a woman who even spoke to other men." Ma Ethelrida said.

"And society and religion want freedom of the woman restricted. It tells you when you marry there are some rules in marriage that is natural and easy to follow. The truth is people will do what satiates their hunger, what seems like fun. And that is how the violence starts. People tell each other pleasing lies and the truth is very shocking. The ego will not allow the truth sometimes. But when what is repressed comes out it is hard and nightmarish to bare." Donna said.

"In Big Jim this awakening to the truth sent him 'murder-suicide' mad. He saw Sherlyn and Jokull as destroyers of his world. I did not know Sherlyn was going to tell him that day. The guilt must have made her sick. She was hurting and she told him. I had to shield her, and she took the baby and hid. He went for Jokull and something- the entity, the iceberg here, captured my son and Sherlyn. It is still a real threat and soon it will consume this whole world starting with this village. Circumstances might have turned out different for Sherlyn, but my son was still pursuing her through the power of that thing. I found her with the baby hiding the next morning. I carried her to church but there were people at the church who was even more demon possessed than Sherlyn. She ran away from the church. The cult there tried to kill her. She was to be sacrificed to their god, the iceberg. I saw Sherlyn ran towards a pirogue that was being untied. She stole it from the fishermen and sped off with the men still trying to hang on to the side of the boat. That was the last time I saw her. I was too weak to save her." She fought to recompose herself, her eyes stung with tears. Ma Ethelrida shakily got out of her chair and took note of the temperature on the thermometer and sighed. It was always abnormally cold now.

"I wish Aunty Sherlyn never came here." Sohpia whispered to Donna.

"The parish priest said there were snakes in his church. He was the last authentic priest here. He warned me about the dangerous people occupying the church, especially Ivar. He told me he was off the see the church authorities on the matter. I think the cult forced him to transfer away. I never saw him again. After he left only the cult would do the mass. But they never let the villagers into their inner circle. And they welcomed the village emptying out."

"And what happened to Jokull and my grandson?" Uncle Bob asked tentatively.

"Not good Bobby. Jokull came for Jude, your grandson, the night after Sherlyn disappeared. I felt guilty about giving up Sherlyn's son to Jokull but he was the boy's real father. Jude was only a year old. He said Brother Aquilo was waiting for him to take them to Venezuela. Brother Aquilo had renounced the cult and wanted to escape them. I learned years afterwards that Ivar had ambushed them and took them to a tanker, which carried them all back to Norway."

"Later I will go down there to have a talk with this Mr. Ivar. Me and David. How many men live in the church normally?"

"A lot of members all armed with swords, and

sometimes they have narcos with them. They have a special relationship with the drug dealers."

"Why would drug dealers come here?" Sophia asked.

"Why not Soph, it's an empty coast here; remote and unprotected. It would be perfect for them." Uncle Bob answered.

"So, it's not safe Uncle for you and David to go there!" Donna said.

"The cult here is just one branch of a bigger organization; called Light and Ice Church. Their history goes back hundreds of years. They flew Jokull and his son to one of their churches. The local group, down by the church, has its funding from the main cult church in Norway. They also give them the connections to be above the law here. They try to communicate with the ice here to gain power for their group. They were sent to the village that August, twenty years ago, because Jokull was a successful experiment; or so they thought that he would be able to draw the ice out into our reality. Jokull is here once again, he came two months ago. But you can't talk to him; he is completely broken by them. For years they had diminished his humanity; until he was their zombie. Now that the signs were right again, they brought him back." Ma Ethelrida detailed to them.

"And Jude? Has he grown up good in Norway?" Donna asked.

"I am sorry Bobby, so sorry. Sherlyn's son, your grandson was murdered two years ago."

"Oh my god! oh no! No! We are so late." Uncle Bob

cried. Ma Ethelrida hugged him and sobbed. Sophia held on to Donna.

"I should have break free and come here." Uncle Bob lamented in tears.

"How did they kill him?" Donna asked with teary eyes.

"He was found dead in a bathtub in a Norway apartment. The Light and Ice Church experimented on him. When he didn't become the abomination they wanted, they slit his wrists and made it look like he committed suicide. Maybe you could not come up Bobby or they would have killed you, with the help of Mary." Ma Ethelrida said.

"When would David come back? He has my gun."

"Last week David and I planned to start a fire in the wooden roof of the church. We planned to light their vans on fire to distract them and then we would burn the church down. Before we got close, one of the narcos called Brent stopped us, but he knew me. He said that was the only reason he let us go. He was the nephew of a taxi driver friend I had, called Mr. Harry. When he was still a boy he rode with his uncle and me, once or twice to Toco. Brent said he didn't want to become a drug dealer but there were no job opportunities for him." Ma Ethelrida explained.

"Ethel, I just want to show that cult what happens when they kill my family!" Uncle Bob said angrily with his tears barely dried.

"The Norwegian newspaper said Jude's death was a suicide, but it was not. It happened on their date for sacrifice. They sacrificed him. Outwardly that group follows catholic doctrine, for a public show, but inwardly they are demonic. They want to set up their own kingdom that with that macabre iceberg as the source of their strength. They made themselves over the centuries into a nefarious, global group. They are obsessed with having their own spiritual age. They believe that the iceberg their god will make them evolve into new beings; with mankind below them, at the level of farm animals, or even worms. They want to be like angels walking the Earth, to have some special superhuman gift, or powers above man. They are down by the church now. The cult will not leave now that there are no villagers to challenge them."

"Why did he let them sacrifice his son? I could never be so brainwashed to do that." Donna asked.

"They are very dangerous people Donna. Their leader is a foul demon. He would bend their will with drugs and voltage to their brains. They knew the iceberg was here since hundreds of years ago. Now they bring Jokull out to sea sometimes to do a ritual, to communicate with the ice. He is sensitive to the ice because of his phobia."

"So Jokull was their only successful experiment. And he is the only way to make contact with the ice. Well we should kidnap him and kill him, so the ice will never come into our reality." Donna suggested.

"We can try but he is well protected. Sherlyn is in the ice alive; I want to free her. Sherlyn loved Jokull maybe she can bring him back from the abyss; he is lost in. Maybe she can stop the freezing that's coming. Bobby you can see her again. But we have to use Jokull to show us the iceberg."

"Aunty did Sherlyn ever talk to Jude through the ice?" Sophia asked.

"After I read the sad news, I told her Jude died; when she came in my dreams. I doubt she got to talk to Jude; since they would mess with his mind like they did to Jokull. And I only now told Bobby because I wanted to tell Bobby face to face." Ma Ethelrida answered.

"The three of us will chaste this cult out. Tomorrow we will drop Donna and Sophia safely back to the car, so they could head back home. I have strong sleeping pills Mary gives me. I never use them but hide them in this glasses case. We'll put them in the food you give that narco you know. You'll tell him it's a thank you for saving your life. It will be warm food so he would eat it right away. When he is knocked out, I will take his weapon and tie him up. Then David and I will light the vans up. When they come running out, we will get Jokull first then shoot their leader." Uncle Bob plotted.

"There are two narcos guarding, we'll have to drug them both." Ma Ethelrida liked Uncle Bob's plan.

"I hope we can snap Jokull out of his bad dream." Uncle Bob said.

"Recently we obtained their bible. One of their members lost it from his truck when his truck broke down the bridge. David fished it out of the water without the truck driver knowing. It was not really a bible though it was a tome with with Light and Ice Church's esoteric creed. It had sagas, skaldic poetry, and a map of Matelot pointing where the iceberg would most likely be found. It had pictures of glowing angelic beings; what the chosen was supposed to ascend to.

Lord Merwittek

Lord Merwittek was a teenager when he started sailing with his father. His father was a brave explorer who sailed from Portugal to Africa. He died of malaria up a river in Africa. Before he died the young Lord Merwittek, using rare stones and gold, channeled his father's spirit into the caravel's compass. Later in life the compass guided Lord Merwittek to a ship near India which he looted for treasure. There he found a hidden parchment with a tree depicted on it. He found out through research that it was a tree that granted wishes and the fruit gave immortality when consumed. When he saw the Amerindian lady using plants to heal people, from deadly plagues, he thought she might be using this tree of immortality. He followed her until he had her canoe by the river mouth. But she tried to kill him and escaped. The fruit would have nourished him, and he would make a wish to live forever by this tree. His researchers could not find the tree over the centuries. But he did not need this tree anymore; the suit he made would protect him from the ravages of time as soon as he could get to it, in his Swiss mountain complex. Lord Merwittek was watching Jokull when he and Sherlyn had seen the iceberg. He had tried to communicate with Jokull, but he couldn't reach Jokull's mind. He knew Jokull was the key to his freedom. Jokull was able to see the surface of the iceberg when Jokull focused his mind. The surface of the iceberg had information that Jokull could use to make a gate to a foreign land. When Jokull left Lord Merwittek started working on his laser light project through the scientists he kept by mind control, in his Swiss mountain complex. With the laser he was hoping to affect the iceberg enough to get free. Twenty years on the laser was now finished but it was untested. His project Aquarius as he called it was well along the way. If it was successful, he would rule the world. He mentally visited his mountain complex. His mood brightened at the sight of his robot army. He was pleased at the chip implanting demonstration. His robots were hideous looking greek myth villains. Some robots had cables that writhed like a knot of snakes; others had bull, tiger, bats or insect heads. Their LED eyes would glow a demon red or cruel green. The robot weapons were part of their arms; machine guns with one caliber bore.

Lord Merwittek's major objective was to come out on top of the chaos that was coming. He wanted to be the one who would bring order after the apocalypse. He knew the iceberg was ready to freeze the Earth. He would say this freezing was his own power and give mankind an ultimatum. To convince them the power was his, he would plant a fake alien signal and fake alien ships in the sky. He wondered if it would fool the world. If everyone obeyed him he could hack their minds and their computers all in one day. He wondered if he chose the right date to start the hoax. He was very superstitious about numbers. He found a lot of meaning in anything numerical. He planned to leave the ice unchecked so it could freeze over the world; and when the population was reduced to the ideal number, he would stop it with his laser. He thought his laser would be very effective in controlling the iceberg. He would be a demigod with a power like that. He would control the population numbers, the laws, the morality and the resources. He would use mind control technologies and army of killer robots. The elites who he could control telepathically would be allowed the most privileges. The labor would be microchiped to ensure that they worked to their deaths. The chips would give him the ability to wipe their mind and program them to do what ever he desired. Whichever survivors were against him would be killed by his robot army. He did not trust humans to fear the ice or fake alien invasion forever. He knew humans had a short memory. There would be those who would secretly want to rebel against him- who would disobey him. When found his robots would deal with them. He made his engineers fit his ship with the special laser. The ship was made some time in the early eighties. It uses one pound of uranium a day to deliver seventy-five thousand horse-powers. It could contain a one hundred and fifty crew.

The Beach

Brent and Danny apprehensively drag the stiff, heavy man-bear off the tray of their van, by its back legs. David was at a safe distance spying them. If it had started breathing suddenly, they might have fainted with fright. The iceberg, Ma Ethelrida spoke about, turned the dogs there into wolves, the trees into cold climate species and this poor monkey into this snowman beast. The plants and animals had changed drastically. David was sorry it was chased out of the forest by the narcos there. The thing was driven to fury at Ma Ethelrida, but it was beautiful creature that didn't deserve to die like that. Brent and Danny shoved it off a steep precipice, where it tumbled stiffly a couple of times, tangling in a bois canoa tree. Brent and Danny snorted more blow to cope with what they saw earlier. Delling had happily paid them one thousand U.S. dollars for the white beast. They watched Dellings apostles drain blood from the poor creature into a large silver chalice. Delling apostles wheeled a great, tall, gilded mirror out. They orientated it to the ocean and where it would catch the poor light. Delling took the chalice and splattered all the blood on the mirror. The mirror frosted cold. Then the mirror glass turned to a transparent sheet of ice. The apostles repeated in a chant "light and ice!" Delling took out his sword and struck the ice pane, shattering it into shards. Then the membership filled the silver chalice with the shards. They would all eat the cursed ice later in a ritual. Brent and Danny were given the job of disposing the carcass. David left Brent and Danny to go on his prowl. It was up to David to gather reconnaissance for him and Ma Ethelrida to form the correct strategy. He passed by the leaning wall of Matelot and stopped the van a little after. He wanted to walk unnoticed pass the group in the church. Who knew how crazy and dangerous they had become? He thought they would kill him if they only knew him and Ma Ethelrida talked all the time about the iceberg. They did not believe in guns, but they were always ready to use their swords. He thought he heard some wolves in the abandon mini market shop he passed. But he saw nothing when he looked through one of the broken windows. He wondered how many wolves there were in the village. Panning across the church yard he observed that no cobeauxs were perching on the errie Marian bell tower today; even they have abandoned this place. The church was quiet as he passed but the lights were on. David thought they must be resting for an all-night vigil tonight. He suspected that the wolves might be down by the beach. Maybe he would find them smelling the fish that washed up dead on the shoreline.

He looked for any strange animals, so he could tell Ma Ethelrida exactly what roamed that place. The sunlight was very weak, and the place was darker than it should have been at the time of day. He had my fears about being ambushed while passing the fishing sheds, but he would be ready for wolves or anything, as he had uncle bob's loaded gun. He headed down the grimy stone steps to the beach. He got nostalgic for the hundreds of coral bean - red flowers that once bloomed profusely along the sides of the steps; the weather here had killed them all. The fishing sheds were lifeless; a relief for him. He docked behind the edge of the wall as he spotted the cult assembling on the beach.

The Cult

Delling came with Jokull two months ago because the signs of the iceberg were there. Today a lady called Mary, a minor member, told him her husband had come up there in Matelot to see Ma Ethelrida. He thought that an old man and a witch couldn't stop him. No one would stop him from receiving the gifts from his God. Mary was just a profane; a useful idiot not worthy enough to be invited, up to Matelot. Delling decided she would not witness the coming of God. He would not invite outsiders to this elevation of consciousness; they were unfit like mud. Delling was a short haughty man with petite build and enormous coveting eyes. He had squandered his younger years in deep malaise of drug addiction. Still a secret council decided to clean him up, and forcefully groom him for the mantle of leadership; as the former head or Light and Ice Church had become terminally ill.

Twenty years ago, he assumed the leadership of the Light and Ice Church. Delling was destined to be head of this cult group since birth. His lineage could be traced directly to the first Vikings who saw the iceberg in Matelot. To preserve his leadership, he deceived people with his charms; pretending to be trustworthy. However, when people opened up to him, and they did quickly, he would use their vulnerabilities to gain control. This was his modus operandi. He deceived people to show their weakness to him and then he gladly enslaved them. It was time for him and the rest of the Order to ascend from their lowly material form into their higher self. He thought soon his success will be so great he would be flying high over all the petty concerns of humanity; no more hunger, no more pain and no more fear of the dark. He was always afraid of darkness so he would always surround himself with light. He had been mind programmed at a young age to fear darkness, and that was how he got his gift. He had a special gift for withstanding high voltages that would normally be fatal. In Norway he discovered he could use his bear flesh to touch very high voltage main wires and channel that power as a weapon. Delling never got electrical shocks like normal people, so he never showed empathy to the members he would shock. Shocking people made him feel almighty. Anyone who did not serve well he would give shock therapy to their cerebrum. Delling told his devotees that he was the incarnation of Prometheus. He donned his LED clothes of glowing cold white light. He wore a long, fibre optic, hooded robe. He strutted in glowing shoes. A white top hat with a glowing halo band he pulled slightly back over his crown. He even donned glowing earrings, rings, and a crystal pendant on his chain. He allowed everyone else grey hooded robes with just a small glowing crystal pendant. They were all armed with their swords. Delling ordered the most muscular initiates to pull his power source; a long, heavy, live electrical cable from the church to the beach. While he was attached to the cable, they pulled by special conducting gloves, the membership wore huge insulated gloves; to prevent their electrocution. The Silver gloves Delling wore sparked harshly, and had many wires leading to incandescent light bulbs, which more of his members carried with reverence. Down at the beach they assembled in a semicircle around Delling. Behind Delling out in the water there was Jokull in a moored pirogue. They had given Jokull the dried amanita muscaria caps they brought. Delling would make him go into an altered state and bring his God, the iceberg. Jokull rolled the mushroom caps into balls small enough to swallow in one gulp, and then he choked it down. He lay in the pirogue as the membership waited for an apparition of God. Jokull's hippocampus gate was opened. He remembered being tortured as a child by his guardians; to fear ice. It was his destiny to find the iceberg. He only recently returned to Matelot to find light and ice for the cult. He knew he would see the iceberg today. But he could only think of Sherlyn. The woman he met when they first brought him here to see the ice. He remembered she was beautiful, and they loved each other. He still loved her now. But she had varnished. He had been kidnapped and drugged for many years. He could hear her calling like she was close to him. Sherlyn was in the iceberg, but what could he do since he was a slave to Delling and his cult. They could control him like a puppet; make him into an imbecile at will. He wanted to awake again like he was with Sherlyn. Love had made him something more than he was. The first time he saw the ice appear he was with Sherlyn. He had sneaked her unto his boat to go to a lonely cove. That day they made love and his son was conceived. He remembered he had a son. He remembered his son was sacrificed. He knew his son's killers; some of them were with him now in Matelot. He wanted revenge but could barely move his own body. For years he was not allowed to remember much. He remembered Brother Aquilo eventually escaped again, never to be recaptured. He spent years in the dungeons of Light and Ice. He heard Delling saying "light and ice, light and ice."

The iceberg soon appeared to the entire cult group. Blind as they were, they finally saw something from another dimension. The transfixed group stood on the shore with their grey hooded robes watching the arrival. Delling pointed to the wondrous event happening out in the water. He addressed his flock "our god of light and ice has finally graced his children. This is our virgin contact with the source of wisdom and ice. It is a dream that left a higher realm to become real to us, its Earthly creation. We have sought it for centuries. Tried to win its favor and finally it came for us." Jokull felt even more hatred for this cult. Delling murdered his son. Delling was a sadistic, brain imbalanced, narcissist and killer. If Jokul were ever allowed to move one finger again he would revenge his son Jude. He would make the cult pay for destroying his life. Jokull knew the history the cult and they did not deserve to meet this powerful entity. *An Amerindian Shaman was following a magical hummingbird for weeks. It told the Shaman to fast and ingest some entheogenic plants, which he obeyed. When he lost the hummingbird, he was far north from where he had landed his canoe weeks ago. In an altered state, in matelot bay, he saw the iceberg and went to it with his canoe. The iceberg had a cavern which he crawled in to enter. The iceberg was a portal for him, he left Matelot and he came out on the coast of Greenland. He lost the way back to the portal because of all the pieces of ice there. He saw some Viking men who had been exiled from Norway. The men had committed heinous crimes against their own community. The Vikings had set off maneuvering through and ice field looking for a new home. The capricious north Atlantic had permitted their sea craft to find the eastern side of the frozen island. From that angle there was only sparse vegetation and perilous isolation. Its bleak, frigid domes would have been their grave, so they did not linger there. To increase their chances of survival a desperate exploration of the other side of the island was undertaken. They kept to the coastline, rounding the cape, praying to find an arable valley. The men in the boat were encouraged by the greenery of this side. Their ship landed on the island where the Shaman was. If they saw him as a man, they would have killed him. He thought they would be easier to control if they saw him as an animal. He took control of them telepathically; and they saw him not as his true self but as an arctic fox. He controlled their minds with the little power from the ice he got. He made them rescue him; as they felt pity for a stranded hungry creature. Then he made them take him back to Trinidad. When they reached Trinidad, the Vikings were temporarily made part of the tribe; still under his mind control. The shaman eventually lost his power to control the Vikings minds, when they ate entheogenic plants. The Vikings had awakened to who they were. They kidnapped the shaman and made him show them the way back to where they came from. The shaman guided them back to Matelot where they saw the iceberg. They climbed aboard and came out back in Greenland. When the plants they took wore off they could no longer see the iceberg with its magical portal.*

They eventually left Greenland and went back to their homeland in Norway. A wealthy woman there believed their story and she became founder of the Order here. Her name was Sigrid. She was a widow who had gotten a large inheritance. She sent the men out again with a great Viking ship, but they all perished in a black storm. She raised a great rune stone for them honouring their magical find. She lived her life trying to get to the entity until she was assassinated. The Order continued under a more sinister leadership. While most Vikings fought Christianity, the new head embraced it to serve his own means. His descendants formed the secret order, Light and Ice Church; that seeks the thing here in Matelot. Twenty years ago, they infiltrated a catholic charismatic group and came there.

"Because what would we be without you, oh god of ice and fire, only lost in time, men with low level cunning. Oh God develop us we are so primordial, only worms of this galaxy, only beast with two eyes, two ears, and mouth and little purpose. Only your light and ice could shatter this four-dimensional illusion. Our locomotion and metabolism is for suffering primarily. Tell us oh great deep power the secrets to ascend. Walk us into the corridor of light and ice. While we are inferior forever, you are serenity and enlightenment. Free us from this material prison." Delling praised his God. The members shouted repeatedly "light and ice! Light and ice!" Jokull knew they would not let him wake again. They would leave him unconscious to freeze to death in the pirogue. He knew Delling was only focused on the iceberg; this was his last chance to break Delling's hold on his mind. Jokull felt like he was at the foot of a savage mountain that he had to climb. If he made it to the sumit without falling to his death, then he would get his will back. To revenge Jude, he climbed the perilous sides of the cold mountain with determination. When he reached out into the real world again, he would gruesomely execute Delling.

The Rescue

David saw two huge silhouettes were emerging from the grey water. The forms were huge turtles heaving themselves silently and steadily through the cold, hard sand, towards the steps. These gentle creatures were supposed to be hundreds of miles from Matelot. The frightened creatures were half disorientated by the Matelot's water. He saw the cult was too hypnotized to notice them coming to him. But if they came, with their swords, to kill these poor sea-animals he was ready with his gun. He was thinking to turn these turtles around before they were killed. Then he heard, at the top step, Brent calling him "Watch nah! You duckin me awah?"

He could not go up the steps now as the narcos would have him cornered. Fear stirred in his stomach. He thought he would be safer in the water. He quietly waded into the cold grey water and climbed aboard the Sandbox Tree; his twenty-four-foot pirogue. He started the boat and looked up to Brent and Danny.

They were pointing at something in the water. Not far into the water he saw a big iceberg rising slowly, it was several meters out of the water. The iceberg had an eerie beauty with stripes of emerald like serpents crawling on it. Soon more floating blobs of ice were just appearing spreading across the water in dramatic fashion; meter by meter creating a surreal topography. The light snow which began to fall over the iceberg became swept away by swirling winds towards the beach. It was the first time he saw snow. He thought it would be so cold that he would die. Under the circumstances the snow was so beautiful it almost made him cry. The wind burned his exposed hand and ears. Many arctic birds flew now in their multitudes occasionally diving into the icy water. When David looked back to shore Brent and Danny had ran off and wolves were at the bottom of the steps. Their eyes warned him "Don't follow that iceberg to your death!" David felt compelled to investigate the iceberg and to see if Sherlyn was really there in it; which Ma Ethelrida had told him many times. His hands were burning; vigorously he blew on his hands to warm them. When he exhaled his breath froze in the air before him. The ice in the water creaked and groaned as the pirogue grated against it. The pirogue would be leaking by the time he reached the iceberg.

Was it this iceberg that made all the nightmares of the village? he thought. Up close the iceberg glistened with its crystalline poison. He anchored the boat and carefully climbed upon the iceberg. He thought *if life was just material and rational then what was this doing manifesting here in the middle of a warm Caribbean region.*

He was startled to see Sherlyn's body, like a mummy; trapped under a thin sheath of ice. She looked alive, and very beautiful. She was in a deep sleep. He shouted at her "hello! Hello, miss!", until he croaked the words. He took his knife from his pocket and tried to chisel away some of the ice, but it was harder than natural ice. He pulled up his anchor and tried to dig the ice with the prong, but he couldn't scratch it. He had Uncle Bob's handgun and wondered if he should shoot the ice. He even thought about getting his cordless power drill in the van to pierce the ice. Then he laughed like a lunatic that not even that will bore this. His arms became sore and his hands got raw from trying to dig the ice away. He fell panting on the ice almost drowning in a pool of water. He wiped his face with a soaked sleeve and sprang up distraught.

"What am I doing here, trying to dig out a woman who disappeared twenty year ago?" He told the empty air nervously. The noise of the approaching ship made him turn toward it. Soon as recognition dawned on him that it was heading straight for this iceberg. The huge red bow of the ship soon stopped, rocking the iceberg violently. At first, he waited to meet the men from the ship. He watched the anchor descending down. He watched the mysterious men, in white, snow jackets, climbing down the rope ladder of the ship. But then something about the military type men, in the little motorboat coming to him, made him cautious.

He jumped into his pirogue and kept low. He moved it around opposite to where the men were landing. Someone radioed the ship. A blue laser beam shot from the bow of the behemoth ship onto the ice. The light lasted seconds and then the men, armed with machine guns strapped on their shoulders, climbed onto the ice. They pulled up a yelling man from the ice. He was Lord Merwittek; long time prisoner in the ice. He had obtained great powers in the iceberg. David saw the laser had made the ice melt off Lord Merwittek's body. He wondered if the laser also freed Sherlyn. The men threw a robe over Lord Merwittek and were leading him into their boat when an Amerindian woman grabbed his feet and pulled him into the icy water. She held him under the water and tried to drown him. She only let go of her death grip and swam away; when the men in the boat tried to stab her with their knives under the water. She swum to David's pirogue and climbed in. David saw she was very beautiful and naked; except for a cotton cloth around her waist. He was stunned by her beauty. She had to yell at him to get him out of his trance, so that they could get away from the men. They sped off in the pirogue as they heard machine gun fire behind them. The men were going to board their ship again, with their king, but they heard gunfire. The crew they left on the ship were screaming and firing their guns wildly. There was a monster onboard; half man half wolf, killing everything it came across. This was Big Jim's new form; a cursed creature. He too was released by the laser light. He was looking for blood, and for

Sherlyn's heart to eat. They heard the doomed men cussing on the ship; and their men were dead in no time. The little boat with Lord Merwittek sped away when they saw the beast. Brent and Danny headed to Arima where they had a police friend. But he was not there in the station. They got arrested for drug possession when they were searched. Some laughed at their story, some wanted to beat them up, but no one believed Brent and Danny that Trinidad was freezing.

Kathi

◆◆◆

David and the Amerindian woman avoided the beach where the cult was. Delling and his minions would have captured them. There was too many of them to battle with, so they took their boat through the Matelot River to get inland.

"Miss, it is all coming through the winter apocalypse Ma Ethelrida predicted has begun." David said.

"Did someone you know predicted this snow in Matelot? I am Kathi."

"Yes! Ma Ethelrida, my adopted mother, and we have even prepared for it. I am David."

He focused the woman's beauty rather than how he and Ma Ethelrida were going to stop the powerful iceberg. He was glad the beautiful Amerindian woman was there. He tried to look sure and unafraid of her, even though she looked like a warrior. Many thoughts whirled in his head as he piloted the boat safely around the rocky coastline. He would ask her what Kathi knew about the iceberg. He wondered how he would eventually get Sherlyn out of that iceberg. He thought wildly that maybe she was killed by the gun fire. He reassured himself that Ma Ethelrida would guide him as to what to do. He and Ma Ethelrida had already made a warm sanctuary for this eventuality. Soon He would take them all to the log house and set up warm fires there. He would have to sneak back to his van. Once in his van he would drive to Ma Ethelrida's house. The van would keep everyone safe from the wolves. Now after all the preparation and he was not ready for this, and it confused him.

"Do you know Sherlyn? She was in the iceberg also. I was trying to rescue her when that ship came," David inquired.

"Yes! I saw her. She told me telepathically that she couldn't leave the iceberg, until that beast is gone. It would've killed her." Kathi replied.

"Are you two still human?" David asked anxiously.

"Yes! But we have new powers now, from the ice. I can read your mind David please stop it makes me shy. More important is that I see you want to save your village." Kathi said and smiled at a blushing David.

"Where did you come from?" David probed.

"I grew up Venezuela, but I traveled, up and down the Caribbean chain of islands, and the mainland from Argentina to Mexico. I have been to Aztec, Mayan, Amazon and Inca cities."

"I must look strange to you?"

"Not really! The sugar cane plants talked to other trees who talked to me in the ice. The sugar cane plants said that Africans were brought to Trinidad as slaves, and then Indians came to Trinidad as indentured laborers. Trees from all over the world communicate with each other. The wisest trees lived before the floods. The floods have destroyed all maybe, but I will not give up searching to find any that survived. I didn't expect to see any Amerindian people when I was free from the iceberg. In my young life I saw only horror. My father was put to gruesome torture and killed, my mother was mercilessly hanged, and my sister inhumanly fed to dogs; when she was a baby. I escaped while they killed the other Amerindians, in my village, because I had more abilities than them. I had rare powers even back then. But not enough skills to save the people I loved."

"I'm sorry your people are all but gone here in Trinidad." David said emphatically.

"It was not your fault." Kathi said.

"Have the trees ever seen anything like this winter before?" David inquired.

"Yes, maybe but I haven't gotten to any trees so wise as yet, to ask one of them."

"How do you talk to trees?" David asked.

"My grandmother was not human as you know it. Her people roamed the Earth long before present day humans. The trees before the flood came made that race of beings. The trees sensed the sun changing in fury, they knew the planet they occupied was going to change forever, so they did the only thing they could to survive. They allowed the little apes to come into their forbidden forests so that they could alter their brains with chemicals. In the ape's little brains, they put the great memories of the trees. Eventually the trees engineered these apes into my grandmother's kind. Her people could talk to trees and build great cities. She came out of the iceberg when my grandfather was a young man. They met in Trinidad and fell in love. She learned in the iceberg, when she was trapped, that her people had all perished; when their cities sunk into the Earth, through natural disaster. I am the only one in my family who learned from her how to communicate with the trees. She started training me since I was two years old. Growing up I found little by little I would hear the voices of the trees. Now the trees trust me, and I love them. When I traveled, I knew many tribes and even met emperors. My healing plants traveled great distances to other shamans. Terrible plagues took the tribes and many people died fast. I was trying to help when I was captured in the iceberg. The man who you saw escaping to the ship was also trapped with me."

"Will he help us defeat the curse in this place?"

"No! Never! He is a mass murderer and very dangerous. I remained quiet in the iceberg so he could not read my mind. He is an evil man. He was sure he would find the tree that provided immortality; as soon as he took dominance of our land. I was drowning him the day iceberg captured us. I did not want him to sense me or the other woman there lying in the ice. I had to unbalance his senses. He knows how to use the ice to extend his human realms. He will try to rule the world. Beauty to us is the flowers, the pure river water, even the snow crystals we see on your pirogue. Beauty to him is his hand on and on gripping the neck of the Earth in total control. He is a psychopath that is imbalanced. He will be defeated before he gets this world because the intelligence, we have is superior to his. He has no empathy. His genealogy traces back to monsters who believed in their right to an eternal throne over the rest of mankind."

"How many of you were trapped there in the iceberg?"

"It's complicated, for instance there is a man there that on entering the iceberg split into many different monsters. I could read all their minds that were there with me, in the ice. Sherlyn and I saw all the beasts sprang from the iceberg and unified into one wolf-man. You are lucky it left you alive. It is tormented with rage. The trees speak to me now and tell me it is a recoverable condition. In that beast there's still a human soul encased, still a human heart beating. He constantly hears a wicked mob of village people screaming mocking things in his ears. His ego drives him to madness. He is his own enemy. He lost his own inner self. He never knew it in the first place. He left it unguarded. His true self is in a nocturnal land. He is a shadowy configuration that has to burrow into the deep core of self. He has to splash down into the water to the glassy bottom of the chasm of his soul. He will howl when he finds the rotting deep sea fish that is his being now. There is handrail he can hold on to, provided by the plants, an easy way for him to connect. He will crawl despondent at first oppressed by the truth, but then he will make peace with it. He can still hold on to his humanity. The plant medicine will bring him to his atrophied soul where he can start feeding it. I will help him. I have to find the right plants and prepare them for him."

"Can you really cure the beast?" David asked excitedly.

"Yes! Of course, he will try to kill me, but I will prepare a blow dart to shoot the cure into him."

"I will help you stop that beast so Sherlyn could escape."

"The beast was Sherlyn's husband. Did you know him before?"

"Yes." David was shocked.

"Some trees were brought here by the iceberg. They give me a holistic picture of this arctic transformation of Matelot. They tell a story of lands thousands of miles away. It is good to be so close to the trees and hear them talk again. Their voices are beautiful but sad with this poor light. And the old trees have the most wisdom of all to give." They gathered the plants they needed.

"I am immune to this cold." She said as she saw David looking at her naked body.

She prepared the plants and blow gun and dart. They took the boat back out the river to the sea.

"I feel my people here". Kathi said

"Their energy still lingers. They will also help me. The Shaman will return, he has left a gate to come back through." She said.

"Now you have convinced me that I have the right beliefs. The atheist I was would never accept these sprit realms. That blind period for me then was all science and five senses. I held the idea that I was here by cosmic accident and that life was a bitch; that ends without consequences. I was hopelessly lost in illusion. I feel really awake now to be able to experience all of this." David declared.

Delling

Delling detached from his high voltage power source and dropped the cable to the ground. He was getting ready to walk across the frozen water to the iceberg. He was hesitant because the frozen water hissed and crackled nightmarishly.

"I don't want him to wake again!" he gestured to the blacked out Jokull lying in the pirogue.

"He was just a tool and we are finished with him now." Delling commanded three men to walk a little way across the frozen water to see if it was safe for him. They walked up to the pirogue. What they saw in the boat was not human anymore. Jokull had metamorphed into a brown and bear-sized animal with lethal ivory tusks and armored skin. Jokull raised his head out to curse Delling but only made deep growls and chilling sounds. Jokull flopped in the pirogue until it broke apart. They tried to stab and slash the bull walrus with their swords, but they only bruised Jokull. One of the men foolishly scrambled upon the creature and it turned oh him its tusk through the rider's chest. The ice reddened as he tried to scream. Jokull tasted the blood and he wanted revenge. He tossed the other two men in the air. He wanted to crush Delling's bones with his weight. He wanted to kill them all. Sherlyn left the iceberg and met Jokull. Delling heard the wolfman on the ship growl fiercely. Delling could not go to the iceberg now, because of the beast on the ship and the bull walrus, which was Jokull.

"We must stop these lowly savages! We are the chosen ones of this age. We want to leave behind the physical shell. We want to be above the filthy level of these fiends. We will give our lives to destroy them. What can the physical world offer me now I'm in the presence of God? The Order of Light and Ice kingdom is at hand." Delling paused as his members chanted "Light and Ice!"

"This is the work of Ma Ethelrida. She can make these abominable forms. She is the cause this evil metamorphosis. She is what separates us from our God. She is the mother of these monstrosities. Bring her here; she will control the beasts so that they will not cause harm to me. Then we will cut their throats and offer their blood to God. Ivar take twenty men with you to capture the hag. I will stay here on the beach with the rest of the group. Go now!"

Sherlyn calmed Jokull by stroking his walrus side. I want to help you grieve and survive our son's death because it's not too late. I want you to hold me in your arms and help me. Don't let their dark arts win. I am here waiting on you." Sherlyn was in tears. Jokull turned away from slaughtering the cult group. He wanted to be human and try to rebuild his life. He wanted to experience again the love he had for Sherlyn. He saw the wolfman coming off the ship as a mist towards Sherlyn. Sherlyns legs were shaking as she anticipated Big Jim's hate filled expression. She knew soon Big Jim, in his beast form, would reach her. She feared his lethal claws that could rip her beating heart out. Jokull transformed back to a man again. Jokull hugged Sherlyn. He held her as if he feared Sherlyn would be dragged back into the iceberg. He tried to console her "I swear neither the mind control nor this winter will not obliterate love, our human experience, or self-realization. Our love was true; against the odds we are in each other arms again. I heard your prayers on in my dark confinement and it kept me alive. If death comes, I know we shall meet again, all three of us, in a better world." Jokull wiped tears from her eyes.

The Vision

A state of emergency was called in Trinidad and a dusk until dawn curfew was imposed nationwide. The violent protests against the police had spread to a couple towns in Trinidad. All the soldiers from the bridge at Shark River were also called to help the police with the unrest. These protests had a hint of treachery behind it; as if it was organized and paid for to destabilize Trinidad. There was a shady group who had capitalized on the little chaos in Morvant to create carnage for the country. The wind blew creepy noises around the house. Ma Ethelrida burned one of her calming homemade incense in the corner of the room. It made Donna and Sophia fall asleep on the couch. She pressed her finger to her lips and led Uncle Bob into her bedroom. There was a small iron bed, jammed to the northern wall, with a coconut fiber mattress, sheeted with a simple lilac bed linen. She would sleep on the free side of the bed and the other had books stacked up three or four height crammed to the wall. She had wooded shelves over the bed with a hundred or more brown little glass bottles containing various exotic botanicals.

"Relax nah Bobby. Here, take piece ah this nah!" She offered him a mouthful of sweet honeycomb. A swam of bees made their hive on a rare poisonous tree and now the honey had aphrodisiac effects.

"What does the most beautiful woman in the village want with an old clumsy kisser like me?" Uncle Bob gazed as Ma Ethelrida shakily unbuttoned her dress.

"For a short time, I can make you young again." Ma Ethelrida said shyly as honey dripped on her breast. The magic honey awakened forgotten tastes. Her wrinkled skin smoothed until she looked twenty again. Uncle Bob fought between the bewitchment of her invading lust and the moving Earth below his feet. Uncle Bob heard the rain begin to patter, on the rusty galvanize roof. As he kissed her the roof leaked water through a nail hole unto their embaced bodies. The rain water tasted like wine on her breast. He rubbed her warm body and his hands grew younger before his eyes. She helped him get naked pulling carefree at his garments, some buttons pitched and rolled below the little bed. Uncle Bob remembered they were lying on the bed and then he was in a different time and place. He and his woman were making a new sacred oath, to honor; love and stay together, until God would call them away. It was a marriage that lasted what seems to be a lifetime to Uncle Bob. He picked her delicious fruits and set her free of her past pains. Her hand reached and squeezed his naked buttocks and her skin became old again. They returned to their original form. Donna had woken up and she asked for David, but he had not returned.

Ma Ethelrida walked to the kitchen window and sighted the red ship and the snow that was falling. The falling snow made her very sad how grey and cold her village had become.

'David better come back quickly.' She said to Uncle Bob.

They would use David's house. He had built a house for this disaster. It had thick log walls and a fireplace. David used logs from the alien species of trees that began to appear here. Ma Ethelrida had the winter clothes and David had the house. Donna and Sophia hastily picked out their windbreakers, and warm clothing from Ma Ethelrida's paper barrel. In front of her wardrobe mirror they gratefully pulled the clothes on in layers over their freezing bodies. The house they were in was designed for tropical weather- rainy and dry, season. And so, the wooden boards offered little comfort from the cold. They had already taken the steel water drum from the yard. They emptied it and placed it in the front room they had eaten in. Uncle Bob started the fire in the barrel; with coals dry sugar cane stalk and cocoyea brooms and coconut fiber from a matress. The weather outside would be deadly cold soon.

"I don't want to die here." Sophia cried. "It will be across the entire Earth." Ma Ethelrida said sadly. All of them were worried and frightened.

The grey robes gathered around Ma Ethelrida's

house. The cult group from the beach reached her. Donna saw them first. She and Sophia and hid in wardrobe. They all carried torches. Fire made their faces red.

The Beast

David and Kathi reached Ma Ethelrida's yard. Kathi left David there. They saw the cult group coming up to Ma Ethelridas house. Kathi promised David that the wolves would help him to fight the cult. Kathi went on to the beach to try to cure Big Jim's desperate condition. She felt his healing had a part to play in the grand scheme of things. David stayed to take Ma Ethelrida and her guests to the warm log house he had. When Kathi reached the beach, she saw the beast she had to cure; it was in the blue mist drifting down to the shore, where Jokull and Sherlyn stood hugging each other. She ran down to meet them. Sherlyn and Jokull beheld a tall, grotesque wolf man with yellow eyes. It growled at them on the gloomy shore. The wolf cursed the man and woman he smelled. He came to make their blood spray and bone splinter.

"grrhhhl! Everything she swore to me was a lie. She is mine but you wretch stole her." the wolf-man spat out these words with blazing eyes.

"You murdered so much until you murdered

yourself. Go ahead kill me for loving Sherlyn. You're a fool. I was entirely malleable to a cult, who tortured me, and she brought me hope and freedom. You only have chains and walls to imprison the true parts of her. Let her free you from this beast form like she freed me. Begin to forgive us." Jokull said with a shaking voice.

The beast shook on the ground holding his head; protecting his ears from the acid words. He rose to his full height and spat out "for the dream that you stole, liar, I will snatch out your breath."

"My mind was not always my own. It was wounded by these fanatics. I went back in my past subconscious and saved my own self as a child. We want to help you to do the same." Jokull cried.

The beast roared and grabbed Jokull's neck. He lifted Jokull with one hand and snapped his neck. Sherlyn screamed and dropped on her knees. "Come on demon!" she shouted. She picked up a sword from the ground, which belonged to one of the slain cult members. The beast grabbed her hair and she thrashed the sword wildly against her attacker. Kathi was close enough now and she shot Big Jim with her blow pipe. The dart was dipped in her special healing potion. The medicine took effect instantly and the wolfman ran screaming morphing into a black rushing shadow.

"I thought I die here." Sherlyn lamented. The Amerindian woman helped Sherlyn to stand. They all startled as they heard the walls of the church crashing down one by one. The beast was in a confusion of panic destroying the church as he crashed about.

Delling had seen the beast racing to the church. He heard with terror the din as the church was desecrated by the beast. He knew his future was in the iceberg and there was nothing remaining in the world for him. He was in the glimmer of the iceberg and had to get in. Then he would escape the fallen civilization he was in. He began to chuckle as he imagined his body becoming more ethereal. The iceberg poured madness into his veins. Now that the beast could not impede him, he ran wildly, with his small group, across the snow to the iceberg; which was the realm of God.

They all felt an earthquake as ancient sacred rocks came up cracking through the floor of the ruined church. The church was built on the sacred site that the Shaman had made when he returned from Greenland. The site surfaced with the Shaman. The Shaman grabbed hold of the beast. Big Jim began to hallucinate. Big Jim saw a full radiant silver moon. He heard electric guitar unison bends played with heavy distortion. The notes induced profound despair in him and stirred up the shimmering dust of the moon. A hideous moon waxed; the top half made of leprous skin and the bottom was molten metal. He saw that strange moon transition to a piceous globe. His peripheral vision picked up a silver wire looping over his head. He felt the wire tighten around his neck and pulled tight from the back. He grabbed his throat in a state of semi suffocation. He lucidly tried to wake himself from the dream. Still dreaming he appeared in a cell. His knee was in sickening pain and looked deformed. His foot was locked in iron. Claustrophobia made him want to plea with his captures for release. When he tried to speak to them, he only managed lupine barks and growls. He heard voices say, 'half man half wolf.' In reality he wrestled with the Shaman until he had collapsed.

Sherlyn and Kathi dragged Jokull's body on top of the broken boat. Then they heaped the pieces of boat unto it to make a bier.

"The Shaman has come to save Big Jim." Kathi said.

"What for? I will have to kill him then!"

"If you kill Big Jim the iceberg will make sure we are forgotten. If you find forgiveness something, good, will find us." Kathi replied.

"Why him? I hate him! I just want to kill this asshole! Please just let me." Sherlyn protested.

"There will be ramifications if you murder him. Don't feed the iceberg toxic energy. Show it how big your heart is. Show the ice that you can love, sacrifice and forgive. It is a recondite body we have to fill with good spirits." Kathi said.

"You were in the ice with me, so you know its nature. But I can't stop wanting to chop his head off with this sword." Sherlyn said.

Kathi pleaded for her to give up her revenge. "You will make this ice shell hideously deform and no one will come for it. Let the ice be free to leave here. The Earth is not its true home. The Shaman is waiting for you to finish cure Big Jim. Because Big Jim took this beast form his blood became a repository of our lost human relatives. There were old species that knew the iceberg better than us; like some Neanderthals. They kept more in harmony with it. In desperate times they used it to survive their furious mother planet. If Big Jim could transition from this lost blood to sentient comet he can lift the iceberg away from the Earth." Sherlyn dropped her sword, which she wanted to revenge Jokull with.

"If this is the price for the world to survive, I will do my part." She said to Kathi with tears running down her face.

She knelt over the sleeping Big Jim and spoke "I will tell you about the beginning of the end between us, before you leave me alone; because the flames of our tripods are now out. I speak boldly my mind now, but it was not always so, as you know. I will tell you about the day I realized my helplessness. That January Ma Ethelrida's plants were neglected long enough, and I was tired of seeing them in the same arrangement. The thorn-less crown of thorns towering over the mini dracaena plants, the bold crotons with the completely dark green leaved mini ixoras, etc. I had impatiently moved all the plants out of their spots to sweep. The chilly breeze made its own mischievous, little swirling heaps of the dried, noisy, brittle leaves. It was almost time for you to return home from work. I wondered if our lives would ever be ordinary again because I had an affair and you didn't know as yet. I brought a smile to your face, as I normal do. There was the moment we were face to face, kissing, when you arrived. My hair blew on my perfumed neck. The white floral of my fifth avenue perfume had long gone out like fireworks, and the spicy nutmeg faded, only the animal musk notes were left. But as I swept and rearrange, when you left me in the yard, the happiness on my face was the memories of Jokull. I was lost in my thoughts. I was trying to sooth my mind wondering why I had become this insincere being. I am not the thief of hearts you think. My love for you ended simply but I did not say. I should have left with my father when he visited us then. You usually came back from work and liming so confused like you didn't know me. I was wrong since I feigned to be your favorite girl; while I deceived to keep you in a good mood. I put on a persona submissive and naïve when I should have been more honest. I had fallen in love with Jokull; it was only natural since I spent my time with Jokull while you were gone. I have no hatred for you. I don't refuse to help you in this dark winter. If all this ever repeats in another life, when you at last reach home, then I would think straight, about the hurt I was causing you. I would be brave and true. I would remember the terrible role I played in the destruction of your life and beg you not to become this monster. Sorry but be at peace Jimmy." Kathi and the Shaman stayed with Big Jim, while Sherlyn went to Lord Merwittek's ship.

The Flames

They heard Ivar shouting "Witch! Witch! come out! Do you believe in light and ice?"

"She is not ah witch! Yuh Crazy ass!" Uncle Bob retorted with a roar. Ivar spat at that.

"I did not turn anyone to a beast. You fanatics spread manure with your lies. The thing you worship as a god makes all these things manifest. It is not a god but a weapon to destroy worlds. It has to freeze us all to death, and your foolish guru to."

The members cried "blasphemy! Blasphemy!"

"I'll stop your witch gob. I'll cut your foul tongue out." Ivar threatened.

"The planet is freezing over knuckleheads! Why don't you save yourselves instead of talking poo?" Uncle Bob asked.

"What do you unbelievers know about our spiritual ascension? I'm gonna put a sword through this witch!" Ivar screamed angrily.

The wolves were watching nearby waiting to attack

the cult group, which Kathi commanded them to do telepathically. One by one they leap viciously on the cult members. Some of the members got their necks torn apart. David emptied the gun on the members through a window. Ivar ran up the porch. He tried to charge through the door, but Donna slammed it fast and his sword hand got caught between the door and frame. Donna jammed her shoulder against the door with all her might. The sword dropped from his hand as he yelled. Uncle Bob picked up the sword and as Donna moved, and the door flung open, he drove the sword into Ivar's belly. Uncle Bob ran out of the house fighting with the sword. David and Ma Ethelrida picked up swords and were fighting. Some cult members managed to pelt their grenades into the house. Donna and Sophia were hit with the Molotov cocktails and perished in the blaze. David chased the last of the cult members off. The yard was full of bloodied bodies, ash and snow. He and Uncle Bob helped drag away Ma Ethelrida, who was screaming in agony. She could not bear the horrible deaths of Donna and Sophia. Holding his hand out in front of him, David led them down to the road. They wrenched their boots from the snow as they trudged on; like the hunters in Pieter Bruegel's painting. Their flapping clothes felt inadequate; even their very insides were cold now. The chill affected their gaits, because these were Scandinavian winds instead of Caribbean breezes blowing. Their exposed faces were spotted with ice. Their eyes strained through the haze of snow to see ahead. They headed to the log cabin.

Sherlyn climbed up a ladder at the side of the ship. On the deck bodies were ripped apart. She found the communication room. She tried to tell the local media, disaster management agencies and religious heads about the deadly winter soon to spread from Matelot. Then she realized Lord Merwittek's turned on cloaking device on his ship, which was concealing Matelot; so, no one would locate the real source of the vicious freezing. He was using his laser and the power of the ice to hide the snowstorm in Matelot. A helicopter flying over Matelot would see all as normal, and no one could send or receive signals. She could not figure out in time how to take control of the ship's main computer. She could not send her message, so people did not evacuate Trindad. People in Trinidad became terrified late Friday night of the bizarre coldness, the ungodly howl of the freezing winds and the gloomy darkness of the place. But they lit fires indoors and nailed carpets to walls to keep warm. Stores with winter clothing were broken into and emptied. People filled the churches, mosques and temples, and prayed for their country. She had to stop the iceberg from freezing the world and everyone she loved. The ice had long been the source of her reality; for twenty years she had been trapped. She had more than five senses now after being held in the ice. Experiencing the effects of this alien realm, she had more advanced intelligence than any other human. She questioned if she had her own will intact now or was, she the iceberg's agent- in some unknown plan for humanity. She would hate to know that she was betraying everyone. She hoped she and Kathi made the right choice about Big Jim. She thought *I think I can't stop this, but it's the end of the world if I don't. I have been trying to figure a way to shut the entity down, but nothing will. I don't want to fail.*

False Messiah

I f he attempted to rule the world, solely as a robot, governments and groups would still try to kill him.

"But if I pretended to be a robot made by all powerful aliens, everyone would think their weapons were useless against me. If they thought advance extraterrestrials were supporting me no one would dare stand up to me. And with my telepathic abilities and experiences of this ice, I would be God!"

He put the chunks of ice, from the iceberg, as an energy core for the space suit. He knew the pieces would also serve to boost his intelligence, because of the knowledge they stored. The noble man shoved one hand on the energy core and the other skillfully darted about his keyboard. His speed and dexterity looked machine-like; some of the powers from the cursed anomaly in Matelot. Lord Merwittek uploaded himself to the space suit that he built. The suit looked like a twenty feet tall, golden Icarus. It had scaled armour and a pair of wings; of a soft and strong membrane, that hung like a reflective shawl. There was a laser in the middle of the forehead, a mini version of the one he made to control the ice. This suit would give him immortality. This suit was the tree of immortality that he had long sought. It would take him through long deep space journeys. As soon as he ruled the world, he would use all its resources to build a ship for his robot body. He got up and carried his former body to its cryogenic tank. He wasn't sure if he could get back into that fragile body again. The suit had everything built in; weapons, tools, nanoscale robots, and a limitless energy source. It would all be run by his brain. The suit was capable of flight and invisibility. He was disappointed that he did not see the Amerindian woman's attack coming. He could have drowned and died and lost everything. He wondered how she was able to block his mind. She and the wolf creature might survive the ice and be a treat to him. He wondered if he could control the ice sufficiently. He would have to stop the freezing ice eventually to start his work on the spaceship. With his men he had escaped Trinidad, flown to England, and then to his base in Switzerland. In his mountain complex waited some important allies to meet him. He ignored most of them- the scientists, inventors, philanthropists, entrepreneurs, spiritual leaders, banking executives, and men and women in the field of biotech, media, energy, and health care. Time was too short to watch these fools stand in. These people found him through connections on the dark internet. He had to send an alien signal to mankind, and also make an alien mothership appear in the sky, in each big city. He would use the laser on The Red to make the iceberg create the alien holograms. The alien signal would come from an old lost spacecraft. In 1999 Earth lost control of a space probe. It was left aimlessly cruising space. It had planned a trajectory completely through the heliosphere. The space probe's primary mission had been to observe gamma ray events. At one hundred and ten astronomical units it trained its telescope on a Gamma ray burst, which could even be seen from Earth with unaided eyes. The ships computer began to compute the co-ordinates of the event and then its equipment malfunctioned. It sent an alarm signal back to Earth that took thirty-two hours to reach the Earth base. And when it did programmers could not figure out how to reprogram the ship to work again. The alchemist would now use this ship for his deception. He would use this space probe to send his fake alien message. The message Earth received would be that the aliens had been lingering on the sun- recording its wobbling and blinking.

They saw the planets and became interested in colonizing the solar system. That Most of the life on Earth would be frozen to death if the noble was not the chosen as Earth's ruler. He would organize the planet- make the nations to submit. Everyone would have to bow to his rule, or the aliens would freeze the Earth forever. Superpowers had changed since he was trap in the iceberg. The world had new superpowers like America, Russia and China. But he was able to keep up with the changes telepathically through the secret order he created on the outside. He was trapped for three hundred years before he learned to effectively communicate with the outside world. He influenced politicians, bankers, high ranking military personnel, pharmaceutical officials, scientist, and religious leaders. He knew there once was a Spanish war with France, about rebellions within Spain, and about the Spanish American war, and the fall of the Spanish empire. He decided to set up his organization in Switzerland. He knew the day he would be free of the ice he would be taken there by his men. In his brain, like a thunderstorm, beautiful algorithms flashed across, and out came the data in many qubits; he took control of the crippled ship's computer. His was a terrible privilege to have, to deceive the whole world. He had to circumvent protection devices and dupe NASA's deep space network. When their computers were under his control, he had to send a fake a radio transmission claiming its origin to be from a retired deep space craft. His intention was to convince NASA that an alien race had sent a message to Earth using the antennas of the 1999 ship- one of Earth's early plutonium powered space craft. They would find his message standing out against all the space noise, and they would think it was an alien race. He also had inside help there should anything go wrong. Part of the message he sent was in the universal language mathematics, and of tones whose frequencies was reduced by a factor to make it audible. He knew he had powers but not how much exactly, and what were his limits out of the ice. He was convinced this was his own will and not a game of the iceberg.

"But who knew how things would end for the inhabitants of this fragile blue planet called Earth. What if I can't stop the freezing?"

It was time to meet the important men he had summoned- the lucky few that would be alive to serve him. The rest of the world would freeze. "This lot will be easy to control but to reach majority of mankind; he would need to lull everyone to a slow brain wave pattern by quieting the Earth." He pondered. They bowed one after the other as they finally saw their master. He addressed the assembled group.

"This meeting is very secret, but we must not fail in this. Win we must, we cannot afford anything else. I have been working hard and my back is against the wall. Its time you pledge your lives to this cause. There will be nothing less and no exceptions. I come into your minds as you already know so you cannot hide. I spent time with the extraterrestrial entities. They have found favor in me. I have made an agreement with them to save the Earth. What I have sacrificed is not important. What the truth is? That I am the only one to save the Earth? All men must obey me there will be a new world order. I will take you out of this confusion, and pain, and loss. The sun will rise again on men. A new era will dawn. They showed me all the wisdom that they know. How they looked, what they are is not important. You have all seen UFO's in your different countries their ship is similar to that. They will communicate to humanity through me. I am the mediator. All you need to know is that through me the human race will receive peace, new knowledge, and a new order. Everything will be done for the greater good of all men. Time is short but we have already built robots that will protect and serve us and destroy our enemies. We will microchip the Earth's population. There must be order that's what the aliens want. If you see I hold up two fingers, but I tell you I hold up ten, and then your reality must change. Do not question and do not be individuals because that would destroy the whole system. It would bring deadly chaos. The masses are zombies, ghosts, or my mannequins. So enough must die and then I will restore Earth. Don't attempt to save anyone committing suicide. They have been misled by individualism, loyalty to family, traditions, national patriotism and religious dogma. The brains controlled by my transmitters will have no problems, only peace I will give. I am not a mere alchemist; I am your God now."

Only he knew that no aliens had made any deals with him to save the Earth. He thought he could control the ice. It was easy to make people digest his poison. He loved this manic period he was having. His ego was in megalomania. He thought nothing could go wrong with his plans. To some the fake ships would seem like Noah's ark. They would stampede in to escape the winter. The atheist would take his enslaving chip because it will save them from freezing. The robot army is for killing people who are not fooled. The transhumanist will fall for the promise of a digital after life- being preserved safely in a computerized data bank. They will look forward to becoming cybernetic. They will think it is unavoidable to be a machine. The rich will be offered the lie cryogenic sleep to be awakened in the future. The alchemist smiled at all his evil plans. He reveled in the freezing devastation. He watched the snow spread up the Caribbean. The storms that came caused car accidents, deaths, and power cuts. Heavy layers of ice covered the streets. Wet, heavy snow was taking down electrical lines. Power lines buckled under the weight of ice and blackout whole countries. Industrial estates were completely shutdown. The remaining electricity utility that was not crippled was voluntarily shot down by renegade general staff, of the utility company. They messaged and made the decision on their own to shut down the electricity. Cell towers were also frozen eventually, and its antennas destroyed; there were no cellular networks in the Caribbean after. The storms havocked Trinidad and Tobago, and moved quickly as far as Dominica, then all the way up to Cuba.

Alien Message

The ham operators soaked in the message they picked up from NASA. The message that Lord Merwittek had sent had been received by NASA. The news was better than any ufo sighting, or any crash site, or animal mutilations. Everyone around their network had vouched for the authenticity of the signal. To them finally this was the most concrete evidence out there for extraterrestrial life. The experts in the field gloated how they had predicted this event years prior.

We are advanced life to creatures of your galaxy. We avidly search the vastness of space and time. We came out of graveyard through a white hole dimensional oddity. You can think of us as self-aware computers who escaped a singularity. We built ourselves in a black hole from other lost mass and energy. We learned how to vibrate and escape disintegration. We will show our existence to you. Our ships will appear to you soon. We are giving a gift to the life on this planet. We have already started freezing your world, because we want a next level of evolution to begin.

We do not invade worlds, we do not eat the living beings, but we often bestow gifts. What we utilize is what you call dark matter and dark energy. We urge mankind to listen calmly. Only united would the members of humanity be given this knowledge; that we disseminate with good will. Make this tiny step forward and quickly your differences worldwide would vanish. There is much power, wisdom, and speed to be gained. You must grow a little to meet the challenge. Do not occupy yourselves with wars; that are scams for profits. Hostility towards other nations is no longer necessary. We will show how to solve Earth's entire crisis. We make the dream happen of safe limitless energy, so you will not pollute the wind, and the water. What could be achieved is simple: a limitless energy source; an end to famine, crime, cancer, aids, wars; and a vast extension of your lifespan. All that we implore you to do is to listen to the commands of our good Lord Merwittek. He is the only one worthy to coordinate this transition to a new world order. You must make him king of all nations; in return for him saving you from this eternal winter. International silence is what we want. We want all major communicating devices on Earth to be swithed off for two of your minutes. Only then we can send Earth our advanced technologies in medecine, physics, chemistry, contruction methods, electronics, and programming. We are very fearful of misinformation. And since it is very specific, we can only send you all of yours dreams in a worldwide electrical blackout. Because if the static interferes with our conversation it would be so cruel for you to listen to, and you will in your subconscious be scarred. Our chosen king for you Lord Merwittek will use his powers to talk to your minds. Do not resist his telepathy as his will is very strong. Do not resist giving him passwords to your computers, as he may need to upgrade systems. Walk in faith, none of us knows the future, and there are good surprises in life, right? All is not bad in your lives. Trust will take you out of the dark night of fears. So, I ask you mankind, to trust that your intelligence holds healing power. We will help unravel your knowledge. You will find parts of yourself, you never thought would be allowed to grow; strive and transcend. And your intelligence will draw near to you, like a magnet, more good visitors like us. Can you already see the beauty of it? But first there must be no transmission except for Lord Merwittek's on am and fm, pirate radio, satellite, internet, cellular networks. All must be left accessible to our chosen messenger. Switch off all your military radars. Our sensitive message is easily affected. All servers must for internet must only be ready for our words. We do not want to lose this great world to darkness but to set it on a course to maturity. But an enamored as we are to you, the offer expires soon. To be exact you have forty-eight hours. We do not linger where we are not wanted. If we can ever prepare you for the weakness of spirit that comes when the chance is lost, we will. Please do not despair people of Earth your peace and rest are so close within your reach. You can start the silence precisely from midnight New York time tonight, we ask for nothing in return, but that the transfer takes place perfectly. The voice in the message was feminine, but the quality reduced almost too robotic tones. The message was translated in all Earthly languages. The NASA team of negotiators had to pass on this message, through diplomatic channels to all nations. The hams agreed that they would lobby to stop the broadcasting any radio waves for the two minutes as requested. They were sure the aliens could solve all of Earth's problems. Space agencies around the world, America, Russia, China, India, Europe would soon have to sign a cooperation agreement. Such an alliance would be far-reaching for man. The framework agreement would be how to unite nations together in the silence needed, to receive the advanced astrophysical and planetary knowledge, new space biology and medicine, navigational maps and spacecraft technology; promised by the aliens. The ufologist among the hams believed in clandestine speeds that could tear space-time and make the abyss of space roar by. They believed just like nations formed the UN to prevent a third world war, the world will join hands to benefit from this great providence. The hams agreed that simply humankind cannot afford to miss this opportunity. The international assembly of leaders took place quickly as the message was spread. At first there was promise that every sovereign state would agree. However soon it was apparent Earth could not come to agreement. Many nations took occasion to accuse, and voice their mistrust of America, and many were in turn treated as rouge nations by the U.S. Brave men didn't want to leave their nations unprotected, it went against their instincts. A place couldn't be agreed upon to receive the signal, from Lord Merwittek, and dissolution was a real possibility. By the time the destructive winter took precedence over the international fiasco, it was too late. The media started broadcasting the alien invasion. It played incessantly. It spread the fear in the hearts of all. People were convinced they would never see summer again. Many believed the promise of a new world order by the aliens. A small number of people were convinced that their leaders couldn't agree on global strategy. And the uncertainty started the breakdown of civilization. It would be the end for all life if the iceberg entity did not stop. The talking heads on the news channesl discussed "No one thought the world would end by ice; since there were other apocalyptic scenarios like nuclear holocaust and comet strikes. Who knew mankind's evolution in consciousness was being timed by this planet-destroyer? Cold winds scour the Caribbean, at ninety kilometers per hour, while our politicians fight overpower."

Icarus

✦✦◆✦✦

Sherlyn sat inside The Red late evening watching the special news reports, which was being shared around the world. One report encouraged support for Lord Merwittek, so he could save us from the end times. Another report showed the alchemist in Switzerland calling for calm and giving assurances that he would be a fair and just ruler. As soon as the world corporations agreed to give up their power, he would intervene to stop the ice. They saw the alien ships; it was in the form of huge hovering rock crystal prisms. The top two thirds were clear, and the bottoms of the ships were milky. Icarus wrapped in a serpent creature was the form the milky parts took. The serpent was an opaque white; a four-dimensional sculpture of Lord Merwittek's Earthly timeline. The tail of the serpent was his life spent in Portugal, the fat belly was his time spent trapped in the iceberg, and the small head was his short recent time out of the iceberg. The form could be interpreted as a serpent trying to bite its own tail while Icarus was struggling to keep the head and tail apart; thus, breaking the repeated cycles of Lord Merwittek's birth and death.

Sherlyn shivered when she saw Lord Merwittek's ouroboros. She knew she had to stop his dystopia from being realized. While he used the power of the ice for evil, she would use it for good. Nature works with a limited set of patterns the iceberg had all the patterns. It was a map of all their entire time. She had to find a pattern where the alchemist couldn't escape; where everything could be fixed, and he was unbound from his space suit. Then the iceberg should leave humanity alone; whose simple genes can't find the answers to please the ice.

She gathered up ice from the deck into a pile in front of the ship's computer. She had one hand in the pile and the other one on the keyboard. She got firmware for Lord Merwittek's cameras and used it to hack them. She then got into his network hacked his computer files. She used the voice recognition on his electronics and captured his conversations. She shut off his water pump and cooling systems. She sent her report about Lord Merwittek to some Russian billionaires. She knew they would contact the Russian military and warn them about the false flag alien invasion taking place. She also sent the report to the best American journalists. They would also contact their government agencies and spread Sherlyn's files across the globe. Sherlyn kept the cloak on Matelot. She did not trust the Americans and Russians enough to give them her location. The iceberg's power was too much of a temptation for them not to try to capture it and use it for world domination. She would hide from them as long as she could to protect Matelot, her family and her friends. She knew Lord Merwittek was using The Red's laser to have his fake alien ships hover over major cities. She made sure that the alchemist could not send robots to destroy The Red once she took control of his laser. He screamed when he saw his holograms disappear. The alchemist was furious. He knew someone was on The Red; someone who knew how to read the iceberg. He assumed joint military forces of the world come to protect Sherlyn from his weapons. Soon Russia and United States officials were on the world news exposing the plans of the alchemist. "We know where Lord Merwittek has his base and have agreed in an emergency security meeting to arrest him. He has a unique weather weapon. This weapon is what he has frozen most of the Earth. However, it is not harp at work, or other atmospheric heaters, it is an unknown weapon. He wants to micro chip humans to lower their minds; to worker robots controlled by radio waves. He would let the ice wipe out the population until it was very low. Then he would own the entire planet. We have an anonymous ally who can also use Lord Merwittek's weapon; and the ally has assumed full control of it. This weapon has showed us how fragile our home here on Earth is. It is time to salvage our world now by freeing ourselves of hate, racism, radicalism, etc. We need to spread empathy, tolerance and non-violence. Our perception has not been reality. We should not waiver from reality any longer. If the alchemist succeeds there would slavery for all? The human imagination has to expand vastly if we hope to stop this macabre winter. While men want to be self-reliant and responsible for their own actions, Lord Merwittek wants absolute control." Sherlyn took control of Lord Merwittek's top robot commander. She used it to destroy his cryogenic lab and biological body. She disarmed all his security systems. She used it to open his gates to the agents. She took control of his other robots to help out the siege team. His space suit was able to withstand all the grenades and bullets Sherlyn and the military fired at him. He wanted to fly to The Red and destroy the ship but feared there would be missiles powerful enough to shoot him down. He had to give up the advanced laser on The Red, but he still had a mini one with his suit. He remembered the story of Icarus who flew to close to the sun. He was scrupulous in his suit design to fly through the Van Allen belt. It would have to be perfect if his higher consciousness was to survive the powerful radiation. He knew the suit had enough speed to escape the Earth's gravity. He would come back one day to build his spaceship. The world would be coming for him soon. He flew into the sky to escape arrest. If it wasn't for Sherlyn, his complex would have easily withstood the siege for weeks. He would have taken the elites he invited as hostages; and used them as bargaining chips. He thought about his ignominious defeat. The elites he invited ran out like headless chicken; to be arrested. Sherlyn wouldn't allow Lord Merwittek to escape. She said "if Icarus doesn't want to fly close to the sun, we will bring the sun to Icarus. She used the iceberg's power to pull a plasma stream from the sun. It struck the Earth's magnetic field and increased radiation in the Van Allen belts. The lethal inner belt sped down to Lord Merwittek as he left the Earth. When the wave hit him his electronics, he heard phantom sounds and saw glaring light. His consciousness dwindled to a feeble spark in the space suit. He slumbered back into the cycle of birth and death.

The Comet

On Sunday morning, the second morning after the freezing, Big Jim was cured. The sickness left him like bats whizzing out of a dead hollow tree. Big Jim felt too weak to move his legs. Once he was a powerful wolf, once he was a powerful man; now he was unable to rise and lift his own weight. He clasped his hands on his chest, and only managed to rest his right foot unto left. He felt his chest for fur, but it was much less hairy. He could not identify himself with the beast anymore. He did not know if he could withstand this change, he was experiencing from animal back to man. He was ready to leave the world. There was no more frustration. Time was not real. The way he responded to his world had created his own suffering. He had denied himself everything good just for revenge. He struggled to heal. It was time to focus on his inner self no matter how dark that seemed. His healing began. He would focus on his day to day survival. He felt unconditional love for himself. He felt so lonely before but now felt at one with everything. He was trying to control a mirage; a good sign of increased consciousness. There was another life coming. He would find more ways for love to come in. he would love himself and others better. He could feel the love pulling him up. The wolf-man realizing maya travelled back to God. A dimensional door opened for him to become a better person. Big Jim awoke a human being no longer a wolf-man. The storm stopped and the snow cleared up immediately. The trees started to change back from mostly boreal forest to tropical flower and fauna; there was now sandbox, poui, breadfruit, capok and palm trees. Kathi heard the trees expressing happiness.

"There is hope the trees are returning to normal!" Kathi shouted mirthfully to the shaman. They found a mango tree with ripe long mangoes and were startled by an iguana leaping off a branch. The tree told Kathi to pick its fruits. Kathi filled her sac with ripe mangoes. The shaman told Kathi to carry the mangoes as a message of hope to David and the others.

The Shaman began to sing in his native language. He sang about waiting to see first morning light touch his good canoe. He sang about following a hummingbird to a sacred site.

Military men boarded the ship to capture Sherlyn. They had finally found her ship. And next to the Red was the most marvelous weapon they had ever seen. The men tried to grab her, but she fought with them on until she was free. She jumped off the ship and took off in the ship's tender.

Big Jim walked up to the Shaman "I am not angry anymore. I feel better now. I am not crazy anymore. I just want to live a normal life. I forgive everyone. I hope that Sherlyn and Jokull will be happy together. I don't need anyone but me to make me happy," Big Jim said smiling.

"You crossed an event horizon Big Jim. Your fate is sealed. The iceberg wants you to lift it off this world. You will sacrifice yourself but save the whole world." The Shaman said sternly.

"I felt a bite on my neck when I heard the bad news from Sherlyn. I screamed but no one could hear me. Something took me over that I could not fight. It dragged me around like a puppet. I was so fragile against the demon," Big Jim said shaking like a leaf.

"A force lived through your body; the material world. Through you it entered our world to feed and reign as king, wreaking havoc and chaos," the Sharman rest a hand on Big Jim's shoulder to steady him.

"How can I lift the iceberg off the Earth Shaman? I don't want that wolf in my soul again," Big Jim asked. The Shaman held out to him a piece of ice, he kept from the beach.

"The military will come here soon. They all want the power the iceberg has. But they will only use it to destroy this planet. They have not made the journey you made to become wise. You were once just an ordinary man who couldn't control his temper, but you journeyed through the depths of your heart and survived. You are now a wise, compassionate soul, capable of unconditional love. They are on the Red already. We must hurry! Your transformation will be from beast to man to comet. The jump in consciousness will make them find the Earth. A gate will be created between our world and theirs for them to use. Big Jim transform to a blazing fire, send ripples through the universe. Hold this ice." The Shaman said. As soon as Big Jim took the lump of ice, he turned ashen. Abruptly his whole body was glowing white. He began to shake violently.

Sherlyn and the Shaman watched Big Jim shoot from the top of the cliff to the iceberg as a flaming ball. Then he and the iceberg blasted up to the sky. Ma Ethelrida, David and Uncle Bob stood with the Kathi watching. They craned their heads up in the sky and saw a bright comet rushing by. After eons the iceberg was finally leaving Earth. The advance aliens had found their star freezer. They waited in low Earth orbit to retrieve it.

"I never thought we would survive the storm." Ma Ethelrida reflected. David embraced Kathi and said "you did it! You cured him!"

"We all did our part, starting with Ma Ethelrida." Kathi said. Kathi told Ma Ethelrida "your son had known the pain of a caged animal longing to be free."

"Sherlyn sent me dreams that Big Jim was still alive. Jimmy was a beast there, but I still prayed he would make it out of the ice; able to control his anger. Thank you for curing Big Jim." Ma Ethelrida replied warmly.

"You have to remember the next time you see a

comet in the sky it could be your son brining something to Earth." Kathi said.

The Shaman said farewell to everyone. He was going back to his ancient pool. He walked back to the ruined church yard. The ground fell apart and tumbled hundreds of feet into a deep limestone cave. The Shaman slid down into the cave singing where at the bottom he would find a tidal cave pool. Helicopters circled above and men tried to drop into the cave, but the ground closed back up before they could. Kathi made the trees camouflage her and her friends from the dangerous men.

The aliens, who came for the iceberg, reached out to Sherlyn and she fell into a trance. She felt like her head was disassociated from her body. She became just a pale, skeletal, greenish face with closed eyes, contained inside a clear glass sphere. The sphere she was in floated upon sea swells. The thick clouds above her drifted across sky in the shape of pond ripples. The aliens spoke to Sherlyn "we are sorry for the damages we caused to your world by losing our star freezer. The consequences of Lord Merwittek using the ice's power will play out soon. You survived annihilation from the iceberg but the greatest treat to your existence remains your own kind. They will fight over Lord Merwittek's advanced robot technology. It will lead to a great war on Earth. When you lived in the iceberg you gained heightened perception, you can use this power to help your planet."

"Ok, the freezing of Earth was preempted because you came for your weapon; the iceberg hologram. My question is can we incarnate to advance beings like you or only to Earthly beings?" Sherlyn asked.

"We incarnate failed stars into ringed planets. It makes no sense to make ringed planets into stars. Our consciousness can spread over astronomical distances whereas the human senses reach is a little beyond its puny physical body. Earthlings can only be Earthlings." The Aliens replied.

"Then incarnate Jokull into Lord Merwittek's suit that's floating in space. He or anything you put resembling him will help us." Sherlyn urged the Alien.

"Call him and he will come down in the suit." The Aliens said.

"I feel like I am trapped in someone's surrealist painting now. An ancient electromagnetic field travels in capricious matter called my brain. I know if you really spoke to me my dna would be ripped apart. Maybe I should just be human again and not the next level up." Sherlyn lamented to the Aliens. They showed her entire life in sliced up four-dimensional sculpture. They asked her "all parts are real and can be accessed by your consciousness. Do you want to return to before Big Jim had the bus accident?"

"No, I choose the part where Jokull and I find my father." Sherlyn responded. Kathi told Sherlyn telepathically that they were hiding in the forest. Sherlyn and Jokull found them unharmed. Sherlyn hugged her father, who everyone called, Uncle Bob. She screamed in glee "daddy, daddy!" He could only manage to croak "daughter, how are you alive?" Recognizing Sherlyn startled him into sobbing. They both cried; for the time they lost, for the happiness they now felt, and for how the world had changed so much. Because he loved her Uncle Bob risked everything to make it to Matelot. Uncle Bob said "I still can't believe you are here, in the real world. I would feel your presence each day because I could never forget you. I heard you inside my head crying out to be free. It was impossible for me to believe you were dead."

He told Sherlyn about her mother how she was with the cult. It made her sad; The Order of Light and Ice murdered her son and sucked the life out of her Mother and Jokull. She wondered if her mother had survived the winter. They all hugged and cheered. They ate the mangoes hungrily. Lord Merwittek's was not the last one with ill intentions for mankind. There was a true enlightenment of most of the mankind, but some men's heart remained mean, greedy and altered very little. When the world is threatened again Sherlyn and her crew would be ready to save the world, illuminate minds, give energy and bring hope. Jokull turned on the suit's invisibility cloak powered by the information from the iceberg. They all strapped themselves unto Jokull and flew into the horizon.

Epilogue

Mary had begged Donna's husband, Ted, to take her to Matelot the same evening the snow came. They both froze to death in the storm. There were a lot of losses to lives and property in Trinidad, but the catastrophe made many heroes. People sacrificed their lives for their loved ones, to save children, or groups of strangers. The politicians in Trinidad talked about making a better country from the disaster witnessed. The religious leaders talked about love, brotherhood, God's mercy and sacrifice. The country seemed to be starting again in a good direction after the calamity that had befallen.

The superpowers of Earth accused one another of conspiring with Lord Merwittek to gain world domination. They increased their military spending on the grounds that advanced weapons like Lord Merwittek's robots might fall into the wrong hands. A treaty was signed for each nation to have a chance at researching Lord Merwitteks robots. The world was rife with rumors of war between superpowers.

Scientist would continue with Lord Merwittek's quest to merge man with technology; to be able to travel beyond Earth.

Delling and his small group had climbed into the iceberg and came out into a vast barren desert. Delling realized it was not a reward from their God but cruel damnation. They realized they ended up twelve thousand years back in time. They were lost there forever when the aliens took back the iceberg. Delling was still were blessed with knowledge from iceberg. He would use his new senses to find a way back to his time one day. Twelve years passed before they found mysterious deep fissure in the ground. They went into the fissure and followed a huge tunnel for a mile. They found several deep pools of water. They finally emerged out of a pit that opened to a huge cavern. When they spoke, the sound made them seem to hover out of their physical bodies. Delling led the chant of "light and ice!" and they floated out their body. They passed upward through a narrow granite shaft until they were out in the open again air. Bellow their feet there was a huge stone structure that fell away with the Earth. They travelled to a ringed planet where they found the iceberg.